"You're good at this."

Declan arched a brow. "Why do you sound so surprised?"

"Because your website leaves a lot to be desired. Yet you established your authority from the get-go." Jordan held up a finger. "Made us laugh so we're comfortable in your presence." Another tick of the finger. "And not once have I been bored on this hike."

"Is my website really that bad?" He hadn't updated it in years, which was surely part of why his business was struggling.

She nodded. "It really is, but your guide skills are not."

"Do you think you can help me?"

Her lips quirked up into a grin. "I know I can, Declan Porter. Just you watch."

He recognized the spark in her eyes as a promise. He didn't have the heart to let her know that most people went back on their promises. Trusting another woman wasn't the smartest thing to do. At least Declan wouldn't do something ridiculous like trust Jordan Wood with his heart.

Toni Shiloh is a wife, mom and multipublished Christian contemporary romance author. She writes to bring God glory and to learn more about His goodness. A member of the American Christian Fiction Writers (ACFW) and of the Virginia Chapter, Toni loves connecting with readers via social media. You can learn more about her at tonishiloh.com.

Books by Toni Shiloh

Love Inspired

Visit the Author Profile page at LoveInspired.com.

Winning His Trust

Toni Shiloh

LOVE INSPIRED
INSPIRATIONAL ROMANCE

LOVE INSPIRED®
INSPIRATIONAL ROMANCE

ISBN-13: 978-1-335-58637-7

Winning His Trust

Love Inspired
22 Adelaide St. West, 41st Floor
Toronto, Ontario M5H 4E3, Canada
www.LoveInspired.com

Printed in U.S.A.

A man's heart deviseth his way:
but the Lord directeth his steps.
—*Proverbs* 16:9

To the Author and Finisher of my faith.

Acknowledgments

Thanks to Jaycee Weaver for helping me when my brain felt melted and my hamster in need of an oxygen tank!

Thanks to Andrea Boyd for being an awesome friend and critique partner. Love you!

Thanks to Teresa Tysinger. I cannot thank you enough for the brainstorming session that finally made this story work. Seriously, talking through that and getting your awesome critiques made this book fun to write.

And to my bff writer friend, Sarah Monzon, for always encouraging me and being a faithful friend. Oh, and for The Creamery's name. Love you!

And last, but not least, thank you to my husband and children for putting up with me being stuck in "The Matrix." I love you more than words can say.

Chapter One

❧

I'm telling you, this will help our sales." Jordan Wood stared at her older brother, mentally pleading with her face to convey the right expression to get Michael to agree to her plan.

"Look. I appreciate that you have all these ideas, but this isn't the boutique you were working in." He tossed a sympathetic glance her way. "We run a general store, selling groceries and some clothing items. That's it. We're not changing the way the store functions because you think you have retail experience."

She scoffed.

"I mean managing retail experience," he said.

What he didn't know was that she did. Okay, not actual in-store management experience; however, Jordan had received her bachelor's degree in business with an emphasis in merchandising. Only, Mike and the rest of her siblings had no clue that Jordan had actually finished her degree.

When she'd first made the decision to reenroll at the university, keeping quiet had seemed like the logical first step. Her siblings were always giving her grief about hopping from job to job and losing her scholarship—the reason she hadn't finished her degree before. Not wanting to hear their comments, she'd kept her plans to herself.

After successfully completing the first semester, it had made sense to continue the silence. But right then, Jordan regretted her decision since Michael seemed to believe she was inept. Still, she couldn't bring herself to tell him the truth. Wouldn't it be better to show Mike the depth of her knowledge before breaking out the degree that had only arrived by mail a couple of weeks ago? Mike was big on actions speaking louder than words.

"You won't even consider it?" she asked.

"I have. I simply choose to continue doing business like we've always done. If it's not broke..." His voice trailed off and his shoulders rose in a shrug.

Jordan wanted to argue, but the office phone rang. Mike pointed to it, lifting his brows in question.

She nodded, rising to her feet and muttering under her breath. Big brothers knew how to get under your skin one moment, then uplift you in the next. When Jordan had asked Mike if she could move back home last Christmas, he'd been sweet and totally understanding. Now that she was running the general store—okay, manning the cash register—his compassion seemed to have ebbed. She might as well be after-school hired help instead of a family member who owned a share in the business.

Walking back into the main area of the general store, she scanned the premise, mentally cataloging all the ways she'd like to change the place for the better. *Don't give up.* Surely Mike would acquiesce eventually. All she had to do was keep a smile in place when customers came in and continue to recall all the knowledge she'd gained in her merchandising classes.

Maybe she could get her sister Pippen or her brother Charles to help. Well, Pippen lived in Fayetteville, Arkansas, instead of their hometown of Willow Springs. Even though the drive was only an hour and a half, Pippen didn't come back home that often. At least Charles was local. He worked as a registered nurse at the clinic, and occasionally, manned the store on Saturdays to give Jordan or Mike a break. If she took Charles—affectionately known as Chuck—out to dinner one day and told him why she could

be a benefit to the general store, would he back
her? Surely not *all* of her siblings thought she'd
failed to adult to their standards.

Right, Lord?

Jordan ran a hand down her forearm, then
straightened when the door chimed. "Welcome,"
she called out.

The man had a ball cap over his head and was
looking down at the cutest little boy she'd ever
seen. The boy's brown curls were a riot all over
his head. His golden-brown skin held a youthful glow as his cheeks bunched up, reminiscent
of a chipmunk. The little boy stopped walking
and met her stare.

"You're not Mr. Mike."

The boy's dad looked up and Jordan's breath
hitched. She swallowed. "I'm his sister. Jordan."
Her gaze flicked from the kid to the man standing next to him. She'd know that face anywhere.
"Declan."

He dipped his head as they walked up to the
counter. "Hey, Jordan. Heard you were back."

Declan Porter was a dad? How had she missed
that grapevine news? And not even a new one,
because the little boy had to be about four or
five. She stared at the kid once more. His brown
eyes were so very opposite of Declan's ice blue
ones. Not to mention Declan had blond hair—
at least he had in high school—and though his

skin could be considered tan, it didn't fall in the brown shade of hers and the little boy's.

Say something. "I've been back since Christmas," she said.

Declan nodded.

"Dad, can I go look at the dinosaurs?" The boy pointed to the stand holding plush animals.

"Sure, River." Declan turned to Jordan. "Is Big Mike around?"

She wanted to roll her eyes at her brother's moniker, but more because irritation over their morning meeting still coursed through her. "He's busy with Simplicity Rentals work." The tiny homes they rented out rested on the land behind the general store. "How may I help you?"

Declan rocked back on his heels. "Could I leave a message for Mike? He knows my number, so he can call me back when he gets a chance."

Jordan silently counted to three. "Is this about the store?"

"Yes."

"Then how may *I* help you?" Good grief. Had he been misogynistic in high school? Loners usually thought they were better than others, didn't they?

His face flushed. "I wanted to talk to him about a partnership with the store." The calm tenor of his voice seemed at odds with the fidgety nature of his hands and feet.

She arched an eyebrow. "What kind of partnership?"

"I don't know if you know, but I offer tourists outdoor adventure guides through my business, Porter Adventures. However, I'd like to expand in the area of retail sales. I'm hoping you'd be willing to carry some outdoor equipment and brochures detailing my adventure packages."

Her heart thumped at the idea. Willow Springs was situated between the Ozark Mountains and the Buffalo River in Arkansas, the perfect area to sell camping gear and the like. But would Mike agree? "Do you have a supplier already?"

Declan lifted the ball cap, running a hand through his hair. Without the hat, Jordan could see it was still blond. Only no longer that California blond shade of his youth but something more golden. The top looked a little long, like maybe he was in need of a haircut soon.

Why are you thinking about his hair?

Hadn't she just escaped a drama-filled relationship in which she'd been wrapped up in her ex's good looks and the charm that oozed from him every time he opened his mouth? Now she thanked the good Lord she'd dodged a man who couldn't commit to only one woman. Instead he'd chosen to devote himself to her two childhood best friends turned roommates. Thank goodness Mike had offered her a place to recover from that failed relationship.

"Um, yes, but I don't have any space. My business consists of myself, my website and whatever gear I feel we need for each activity."

Jordan's mind spun different scenarios as she imagined what her brother would say. She needed more information. "What are you wanting to sell?"

"Life jackets, camping gear, accessories for hiking, etcetera." Declan slid his hands into his pockets.

Jordan scanned the inside of the general store, taking in the groceries on her right and the clothing items on her left. Where would they have the room for camping gear and the like? "I'm not even sure where that would all fit."

"Okay, what if we started off small?" Declan rocked on his heels. "Like carrying hiking packs, boots, knives or multitools, maybe even some first aid kits. That shouldn't take up too much room, right?" A hopeful look entered his eyes. "If you decide that's a good fit, we could revisit the bigger items, like tents and sleeping bags."

That all made sense. Plus, she'd been dying to rearrange the store to make it more shopper friendly. She'd taken classes on store layouts, and the general store was a poster child for what not to do. *But it's tradition*. After losing Pop a couple of years ago, Mike seemed to be clinging to the ways of their father. Not that she could blame him, but Pop had always taught them to do things smarter, *not to be* obstinate beyond belief.

She blew out a breath. *Focus, Jay*.

"Do you have a plan? Paperwork or pictures of the items I could see?" Maybe stalling would help her figure out the right path. She didn't know if going into business with Declan was a very good idea for the store *or* for her.

She could recall the time Declan had accused her of being high and mighty and a know-it-all back in high school. Their one blowup had happened in the only class they'd taken together their entire high school career. He'd seemed to dislike her on principle, because it certainly wasn't based on actual knowledge of her. They'd never hung out in a crowd, let alone on a one-on-one basis. He'd kept to himself, then left Willow Springs once they graduated.

Entering the orbit of another possible toxic male was not in her plans. She needed to stay on the straight and narrow and lead a single, drama-free life. Make different choices, because the ones of the past had landed her back in Willow Springs living with her big brother, single and low on funds.

"I have the paperwork in the car." Declan sighed, running a hand over his blond goatee, then glancing at his son. "I'll be right back. Is it okay if I leave him in here?"

His son was humming happily while playing with the plush stuffed animals. "Yes, that's fine." Besides, what could go wrong before Declan got back?

Declan Porter couldn't believe Jordan Wood had really returned to Willow Springs. He'd heard rumors through the gossip mill but chalked it up to just that, *gossip*. He'd been so preoccupied trying to make his business viable that he'd never given credence to the talk. *Guess the town busybodies were right for once.*

He grabbed the folder off the passenger seat, then closed the Jeep door and inhaled deeply, taking time to say another prayer. *Lord God, please let the Woods see a reason to partner with me. You know how much I need this to work.*

The bank wanted proof his business was a success before they considered loaning him the money that would pay back his ex. She'd originally helped him start his business, acting as a silent partner. Now that she'd found someone who made her want to settle down and live a married life, she wanted the money back. Her words, not his. So now he was scrambling to figure out a way to return her investment and make his business more appealing to the suits at the bank on Main Street. Anything to maintain the peace.

The financial stress had Declan wanting to stay outdoors and away from people, but life called. He walked back across the parking lot, taking in the yellow farmhouse. The whole bottom floor was the general store. Behind the building were twelve tiny homes also known as Simplicity Rentals. Tourists—or newcomers who wanted to make Willow Springs their residence—could rent one of the places for a short-or long-term period.

That had to mean the Woods were doing well and could help him. Right? Especially since he heard Mike was building a couple more tiny homes to add to the assortment. Declan was tired of eating PB&Js along with River every single day. If he could bring in more income, then the menu could change for the better. He just knew that working with Mike—or Jordan from what it looked like—was the answer.

Declan opened the door to the store and froze. Jordan knelt before River, grinning and talking as if they were the best of friends. He tried to keep the stone-cold shock off his face, but judging by the cool air coming into his mouth, he failed. Seeing River talking to another woman and laughing was a sight to behold.

"Everything okay?" Declan asked, tugging at the collar of his windbreaker.

"Yes, we were just getting to know each other." Jordon rose. "Did you find the info?" Her snooty tone sounded no different from how she'd spoken back in high school.

Why had he expected anything different? She'd never spared him two glances before, and when she had, her looks were always reminiscent of a person inspecting dirt on their shoes. He got it. He'd been the weird kid with no parents and handmade clothes, thanks to his grandma's desire to be thrifty. His jaw ticked. "Here." He thrust the folder at her, trying to battle old feelings.

Hadn't he worked through all that from the past? He was better now. Plus, he could buy his own clothes—well, after he made sure River was taken care of.

"Dad, Dad." River held up a plush triceratops. "Can I get this? Can I?"

Declan's stomach tensed. He hated telling his son no. "Don't you have enough dinosaurs at home, bud?"

"I don't have the tri'tops though."

He took the plush toy and peeked at the tag. It wasn't much but was more than he'd planned on spending today. Still… "How 'bout I get it for you next time?"

His son's bottom lip trembled. "But I want it now." The last word came out in a whine.

Declan rubbed the top of River's head, moving his son's brown curls back and forth. Times like this, Mekayla's features stood out boldly in River's face. Declan was able to view his son and remember his ex without any bitterness over how their relationship ended. He'd come to terms that Mekayla hadn't wanted to be a wife or a mother, as evident by her ability to walk away without a backward glance.

When he'd first returned to town with River in tow, he'd received many odd looks. Not that he was surprised; their open-eyed stares had merely irritated him. Yes, Declan was white and River half Black, but surely in this day and age, that didn't shock people anymore. Only apparently it did. There was always someone who couldn't help but stare.

Declan blinked, focusing on his son once more. "I know you do, bud." He squatted down. "Remember when I said I can't always buy you things just because you want them?" He couldn't afford to, not to mention there would be no room in their place if Declan gave in to River's every whim.

"Yeah…" He drawled out the word in a petulant tone.

"Well, now is one of those times. But next time we come here, I'll get you something." Maybe he could put off needing to come back here for a bit.

"Promise?" River's puppy dog eyes hit Declan straight in the heart.

"I promise, son."

River nodded and Declan stood, taking his small hand in his.

Jordan shifted and Declan shook his head inwardly. For a moment, he'd forgotten he'd been talking to her. "Um, thanks for taking a look at the paperwork."

"Sure." Jordan waved to the little boy. "I hope you come back and visit." Her almond-shaped eyes studied River.

As her gaze scanned over his son, Declan took the opportunity to see what changes time had brought in her. Jordan's black hair was now in a pixie cut. Her brown skin reminded him of the acorns River had used in his latest craft project from school. The full lips and beguiling dark brown eyes all summed up one thought. Jordan Wood was still undeniably good-looking. *Not that I care.*

River gripped Declan's hand, smiling shyly back at her.

Time to go. Declan headed for the door then paused, hand resting on the knob. "I have a tour tomorrow. How about I call you afterward? See if maybe y'all've come to a decision?"

"Sounds like a plan."

"Thanks."

"Sure."

He exited the store, dragging in an inhale as he walked across the parking lot. How could she still get under his skin? Make him question the words he'd used, the body language he'd presented—every single thing that made up their interaction?

"How come we didn't see Mr. Mike, Dad?"

"Big Mike was busy." And had evidently left the second-oldest Wood sibling running the operation.

His mind still couldn't process her presence. Why'd he have to think of the times he'd wanted to catch her eye? Despite never feeling good enough, he wanted to be noticed by Jordan, the it girl. Which was strange because high school had been an odd time for him. His unconventional upbringing made Declan feel strange around kids his own age. He'd never been able to make friends easily, and girlfriends had been almost nonexistent until he went away to college.

In high school, Jordan had been the one who'd always intrigued him. She rarely interacted with him. He hadn't been sure if that was because their paths didn't really intersect or because she thought herself above him. That weird scrutinizing gaze he'd been on the other end of a time or two seemed to study him like a specimen under the microscope. That couldn't be a good thing.

Declan could only pray that Mike would be the one making the final decisions about the proposed partnership. They weren't really friends, but they were friendlier than the nature of the uneasy interactions he had with the guy's sister. Going to the same church and seeing one another around town helped. Surely Mike would want to help Declan out. Right? Because if Declan had to depend on Willow Springs High's former varsity cheerleader, who knew what would happen to his business, his *life*? A shudder ran through him.

As soon as Declan had a moment to himself, he'd be hitting his knees and begging God to bless him. Banking hope on a woman like Jordan Wood could only land him in the same position he'd been put in by his ex—alone and struggling financially. Certainly not a position Declan wanted to find himself in again.

Chapter Two

A beautiful spring day viewed from the general store's front porch was the perfect way for Jordan to enjoy her lunch break. She took a sip of her coffee—half of it filled with hazelnut creamer—and imagined a world where her dreams had come true. Only problem was, her dreams weren't necessarily concrete. Jordan wanted to work in her field—she had for a brief moment when she'd lived in Fayetteville—and she wanted to make a difference. Beyond that, she hadn't decided what direction to go in.

Working at the fashion boutique had pulled her experience and her degree together in a way that made her giddy to start the day. Well, for those first couple of weeks anyway. Soon it became obvious that fashion—as much as she loved clothes—wasn't where her work passion lay. Suggesting clothing items for customers was only fun when they wanted help. Nine times out of ten, they left dressing rooms a mess and only purchased one item while leaving a giant pile of clothes behind.

Now that Jordan was back home, she wanted a chance to spread her wings. To incorporate the studies she'd read and make the general store better than ever. But Michael refused to see the validity of her suggestions. At least he'd agreed to sell Declan's wares at the request of a tiny profit for the store.

If only Jordan could figure out a way to show Michael how good she was at her job. Not that she was trying to be cocky or anything; she just had a gut feeling that if he let her loose, their profits would soar.

She bit her lip. What if she could find a business to revamp and show as proof of her capabilities? A company who wasn't thriving but had viability. Then she could use them as a test subject, and if—no, *when*—their business improved, Michael would be more willing to listen to her. It would be a success story, and Jordan desperately needed a win after so many losses. Her Pop, her apartment, her friends, her boyfriend—ex. *Ugh*, she didn't care about that last one, unless she wanted to catalog how utterly foolish she'd been in that relationship.

Simply put, Jordan no longer wanted to feel

like a failure. Taking so long to get a bachelor's degree and having so many mistakes in her past had broken something inside of her. She wanted her family to be proud of her. She wanted *Pop* to be proud, even if he didn't have an earthly seat to watch their family business improve.

Her phone chimed.

Declan: I just finished a tour. Could we meet up and discuss my proposal?

Jordan glanced at her watch. She still had forty-five minutes on her break.

Jordan: Sure. I can come by your place in ten.

Declan: Perfect.

He texted her his address, and she went inside, trading her coffee cup for her purse. Then she swung by her brother's office to grab Declan's folder. Mike had added a contract with all the fine print. Her eyes had practically crossed when she'd read it for errors. Due to Mike's meticulous nature, nothing had needed to be changed, simply printed out for signatures.

Her sedan sat in the front parking lot, where all Simplicity renters and general store customers parked. After setting her things on her passenger seat, then buckling in, Jordan pulled out of the lot and headed into town.

Going anywhere in Willow Springs probably meant you'd pass through Main Street en route to your final destination. Today was no different. Jordan took her time traveling down the street, enjoying the floral wreaths dangling from the lampposts and the dogwoods blooming everywhere. The sweet scent of spring wafted through her open window and bolstered her spirits. The scenery slowly went from floral visuals to houses. Soon she pulled up to a brown A-frame.

Her eyebrow arched in surprise. Somehow this wasn't exactly what she'd imagined Declan lived in. She'd envisioned a home in the heart of suburbia. Maybe one of those bungalow-style houses a couple of blocks away from Main Street. Only Declan's place was nestled in the middle of the forested area. Almost like he was alone, despite the neighbors across from him and on either side. How many acres did he own?

Jordan walked up the sidewalk and knocked on the door. It swung open, and Declan stood in a pair of boots, jeans and a plaid shirt.

"Jordan."

She dipped her head, ignoring the guarded feeling that immediately sprang to life. "Declan."

"Come on in."

Her breath hitched as she crossed the threshold. *What's wrong with you? It's just a house.* Yes, but it was the home of the elusive Declan Porter. Crossing the threshold was like being granted access behind the curtain. She followed him down the short hallway that opened up to a great room. A kitchen area situated to the left had an open space with a small dining table situated halfway between the kitchen and living room.

To her right was the sitting area, complete with a brown leather couch that had an orange blanket draped over the back. A wooden coffee table—was that reclaimed wood?—added a rustic appeal to the whole space. She didn't know *what* to think about the rust-colored shag carpet though. It kind of screamed *male-only abode*.

Declan cleared his throat. "Would you like something to drink?"

"No, that's okay." She met his gaze. "I had coffee before I came over. It's my lunch break."

"I didn't know that when I suggested a meetup." He ran a hand through his hair.

"It's fine. I'm the one that suggested coming over now." She shifted her weight to the other foot. "I have a long break, and instead of doing a million things, I decided to relax." She hid a wince. Judging by the chagrined look on his face, her words had only made things worse. "Promise. It's okay. Uh, let's talk business."

She pulled out the folder from her large tote and extended it to him.

"Thanks." He gestured toward the couch, then took a spot in the recliner across from her before opening up the file. "A contract?"

"It protects your interests as well as ours." She bit the inside of her cheek. Did that sound snarky or professional? Despite the strain between them—or was she the only one imagining it?—she *was* going for a business persona.

"Makes sense," he mumbled to himself, eyes skimming the contents.

"I detailed how much space we can offer, even included opportunities for camping gear—"

His gaze shot to hers. "You did?"

"That's what you wanted, right?" Had she misheard him?

Something in his eyes glittered. "Yes. Thank you."

Was he touched? Why did the thought soften something inside her? "The only change put in there is a nominal fee we're requesting for our efforts."

Declan's head jerked up. "How much?"

Jordan licked her lips, shifting her gaze to a spot over his shoulder. Would it be too much for him? She had an inclination he was struggling in the finance department. "Michael thought a ten percent fee would suffice for the retail space, along with you agreeing to advertise Simplicity Rentals with your clients."

"That's fair."

She slouched in her seat. *Oh good.* "Have a look at the paperwork at your leisure. If you agree with everything outlined, sign it and return it to me. We'll go from there."

"Thanks. I really—" Declan broke off at the sound of padded footsteps.

River walked straight toward his father. "I'm hungry." He rubbed his belly, eyes widening with sorrow.

Jordan had to smother a laugh. She'd be a goner if those big brown eyes turned her way with that puppy-dog expression.

"Okay, bud. I'll cut you up an apple in a minute."

River leaned his head against Declan's chest, then froze when he saw Jordan. "You're the pretty lady from the store."

Heat filled her cheeks. Why did her heart and mind feel so embarrassed by the sincerity in the little boy's words? "Thank you so much. I think you're adorable."

"Dad, what does that mean?"

"You're cute," Jordan interjected. She had no

idea what Declan would've said, but that was the simplest explanation she could think of.

River ducked his head and mumbled, "Thank you," softly.

She stood. Time to leave before the little boy turned her armor to rubber. "I should probably let you get back to...life." She mentally berated herself for the lousy word.

"If you give me a minute, I can sign the papers now. I'll send you an email once my distributor lets me know when the first shipment will be in."

"Okay."

He signed the paperwork with a flourish, then passed everything back to her.

"Do you have another tour today?" she asked.

"No. Just had the one scheduled."

She tilted her head. "What happens if someone wants to hire you last minute? Do you ever do that?"

"Uh, no. I need a sitter, so I always have to plan in advance."

"How far in advance?" She held her breath, mind spinning as ideas sprung up like popcorn.

"Enough time to secure a babysitter."

This was it. Porter Adventures could be her pet project.

"I have an idea."

Declan held up a finger, then pointed down

at River. She nodded her understanding and sat back down. She'd wait patiently for him to take care of his son if it meant a chance to convince him to work with her. *Please, please, please.*

That spark in Jordan's eyes had every nerve ending sounding an alarm to potential danger. Declan tried to think of reasons for that strange glint, but River whined about an apple once more.

Declan grabbed the fruit from the crisper and began cutting, careful that any evidence of the core was completely gone from each slice. No way River would touch the snack if he saw an indentation from the seeds. *Kids.*

Back to the issue of Jordan and that gleam in her dark brown gaze. What was she up to? Did she need a tour guide? Declan laughed to himself. Jordan Wood did *not* seem like the type of woman to go traipsing in the great outdoors. He'd need a bucket of popcorn and reclining chair to watch that unfold, and he would enjoy the spectacle fully.

His ex-wife, Mekayla, had never liked the outdoors either. That should have been warning number one that their relationship would end poorly. Only Declan had told himself opposites attract and not everyone had the same hobby. Still, he shouldn't have married a woman who disdained the very thing that helped him navigate this difficult world.

Declan called for River and set a plate before him on the dining table. "Eat up while I talk to Ms. Jordan, 'kay?"

River nodded, already munching on the fruit.

Lord, I don't know what Jordan needs or wants, but please help me navigate any turbulent waters. The unknown always made him a little hesitant, and having Jordan thrown into the mix seemed like a hazardous recipe. The woman attracted attention wherever she went, and Declan needed the opposite to happen. Calm and steady was his mode of operation. Somehow he couldn't imagine the second-oldest Wood sibling liking the peaceful life. She'd been so outgoing in high school, and he had no reason to believe that had changed whatsoever.

Declan sat across from her, resting his elbows on his thighs. "So what's your idea? Do you need a tour guide or something?" He gave himself bonus points for saying that with a straight face.

"No, not at all." She scooted to the edge of the sofa. "I was thinking I could be your personal business consultant. Look at your website and the tour packages you currently offer, then I can give you advice on how to bring in more business. You'll get a—"

"Whoa, whoa, whoa." He waved his hands in the air, head spinning, trying to decipher what she was saying.

"I'm good at this. I promise."

"Good at what? I don't…" What was happening?

"Let me start again," Jordan said, her tone as imploring as the clasped hands before her.

Declan nodded. A do-over would be good.

"I get the feeling your business is struggling." *Understatement.* "It is."

"Okay, so I have a business degree with an emphasis in merchandising. But besides that, I've learned all about branding, marketing, et-cetera."

So far, nothing she said sounded awful, but why did he feel like the other shoe had yet to drop? "What does that have to do with me?"

"Not you specifically but Porter Adventures. I want to show I can turn a failing business around." She winced. "Not that I mean yours is failing."

Oh, but it was. Not that he wanted to admit that out loud.

Jordan continued. "I'll study your website and tour packages, and ask questions about what you want the business to look like. You know, an if-all-your-dreams-came-true type deal. Then I'll take all of that information and come up with a plan to improve your company."

Huh. That didn't actually sound painful. Still… "What's in it for you?"

"I'm so glad you asked." She flashed a grin so quickly it momentarily stunned him. "I'd like to be able to list you in my portfolio of successes."

"That's it?" He scratched his beard.

"Yes. You'll be my first client."

Ah. That was the kicker. "You've never done this before?" He didn't mean to sound skeptical, but seriously. Did she truly expect him to be her test dummy?

"I mean, this may have merely been an exercise in one of my business courses. However, if you mean outside of the university specifically, no."

Declan studied her for a moment as he processed her offer. *God, should I give her a chance?* Though, he didn't really see how he could come out on the losing end. Still, proceeding without that peace in his spirit was a no-no. Experience and previous bad decisions had taught him that. Yet no immediate inkling of God's answer came. Maybe this was one of those good-either-way situations. Besides, his business *was* failing, and Declan needed to show the bank that he was a good risk.

"All right, then. I accept your offer."

Jordan clapped her hands together, cheeks bunching with joy. He couldn't help but note how stunning she was. *Don't go there. Women are off-limits. Been there, have the divorce papers for proof.* Plus, there was River to consider. That alone would ensure Declan treated Jordan as a business associate and nothing more.

"How do we do this?" Declan asked.

"We can plan a time for me to look over any pertinent paperwork you have. I'll go home and review your website." She paused. "I'm assuming it's PorterAdventures.com?"

"It is." That had seemed the logical choice.

"Good. For now, your assignment is to get me any paperwork you feel I need to see. Also, let me know when your gear is set to arrive." She stood.

Declan nodded, coming to his feet as well. "I can do that."

"This is going to be great. Just you wait and see." She waved, then left.

He exhaled and stared at the closed door. What had he just agreed to? Would he come to regret it, like a bunch of his other past choices, or could she really boost his business enough for the bank to give him the loan?

"Dad!" River yelled out.

Declan turned toward the table, but River was

standing with his nose pressed to the French doors. "You okay?"

"Yes, come here. There's a deer in our backyard."

Declan smiled. Everything was an emergency to a five-year-old. At least looking at deer was better than continuing to examine his life choices and finding them lacking. If Jordan couldn't help him, maybe selling gear in their store would. Something had to work, right?

Please Lord. You know my needs. I know You're the Great Provider. Please bless me. Because he needed to be able to provide for River. That was the only thing Declan was concerned about.

Meanwhile, he'd try not to worry about tomorrow and enjoy the blessings of today. Despite the niggling doubt whispering in the back of his mind.

Chapter Three

Declan's website was a hot mess. Jordan couldn't believe it. Not only was it completely basic, but it looked like an elementary student had designed it for a school assignment. She groaned, dropping her head into her hands. How could she kindly tell him the state his site was in?

"This isn't a disaster," she mumbled to herself. "A website fix is an easy one." Even she knew how to create a better web page. And that was a good thing since, most likely, she'd have to do it herself, because she wouldn't make Declan pay out of pocket for her pet project.

Lord God, please guide me. Please help me help Declan. She needed a win so badly. Dropping out of college the first go around, choosing horrible boyfriends—though Traun took the cake—and moving back home equaled failure in her books. Surely God understood the state of her heart and the yearning to be better. *Please*.

Jordan began jotting down next steps in her notebook. She'd need to look up other outdoor adventure guides in Arkansas and see how their webpages looked. Maybe even incorporate some of their tours he wasn't offering, but tailor all the information to Declan's brand. Speaking of which, it didn't appear Porter Adventures had a logo or tagline. She should probably tackle that first. Maybe they could get a logo added to the gear he wanted to sell.

She picked up her cell and dialed Declan's number.

"Hello?"

"Hey, it's Jordan."

"So the caller ID said."

She shook her head despite the twitch of her lips. "Does it really say Jordan, or did you put some horrid nickname for me?"

"Is that what you did to mine?"

She laughed. "No. It says Declan Porter."

"And yours says Jordan. But I'm sure you didn't call to find out how I listed you in my contacts."

"Right." She blinked. "Do you have a logo?"

"For what?"

She bit back a groan. "For your company."

"Oh. No. Why? Should I?"

Lord, grant me strength! "Declan, how long have you been doing this?"

"Four and a half years."

What? She stared at the phone then brought it back up to her ear. "You haven't created a logo or changed your website since then?"

"No," he said cautiously. "I take it you think I should."

"Probably four and a half years ago."

A puff of air greeted her ears. "I don't have money for that."

"That's fine. I'll take care of it."

"Take care of it as in you'll pay for it, or something else?"

Oh boy. She didn't know if Declan meant that to sound snarky. Working with him would definitely fall into the *need patience* category of things she needed to work on. "Don't worry. I won't spend your money. I asked you to do this, so I'll handle things when possible. However, if I can't provide a quality product or afford someone who can, I might ask a smidge from you." Or not get it. At this point, any upgrade was better than the current condition.

"Then thank you."

"Was that so hard?" She slapped a hand over her mouth, squeezing her eyes shut as well. That was supposed to remain a thought.

Only Declan gave a huff of laughter. "You

have no idea. What do you need in order to update my website and create a logo?"

"Do you have a slogan for Porter Adventures? Something you promise your clients?"

"No. Should I?"

Jordan thought fast. "Do you have a tour today?"

"Yes. I'm leading a hike at eleven."

"Perfect. Sign me up."

"Excuse me?"

She rolled her eyes at his incredulous tone. "If I see how you are in nature, I can translate that to a possible slogan for your business. Who knows? I may even take a few pics on my phone that can be used on the site." Not that she was a photographer, but smartphones certainly allowed the novice to look more experienced.

"All right. Should I swing by and pick you up, or do you want to meet at the hike site?"

"I'll meet you there if you text me the information." Good thing it was her day off. Mike shouldn't have a problem if she disappeared for a few hours.

"That I can do."

Wonderful. They were getting somewhere. She said goodbye, then did an internet search on outdoor tour guides. There were tons in the Natural State, which was perfect. The more sites she could study, the better chance she had of making Declan's new webpage user-friendly and appealing to nature lovers. Plus, she wanted it to be on par with the other companies', if not better.

An hour later, Jordan came to her feet, stretching her back. Charles had shown up right on time to open the store this morning while Michael worked on finishing up the build for one of the new tiny homes. Working above store on Declan's company reform had been interesting but also a little monotonous.

Getting outdoors and seeing how Declan handled tourists would be super beneficial. She could come up with a phrase that explained why Declan would be the best adventurer in the area. Not that she believed that per se, but his future customers needed to when they stumbled across his website.

Her eyes widened, and she wrote down *Advertisements* in her notebook under the heading *Things Declan Needs*. There, now she could leave. She looked down at her clothes. *After I change out of my lounge pants.* Good thing she had hiking gear already hanging in her closet.

A short while later, Jordan ran down the stairs leading to the ground floor of the general store. She waved to Charles as he talked to a customer, then crossed to the exit.

Growing up, she'd thought it was so cool that

they'd lived above the store, but now she wondered if it couldn't be used to host another level of goods to sell. Then again, where would she and Michael live if they did that?

The tiny homes.

She scrunched up her nose. They were adorable, but she didn't want to be relegated to two-hundred square feet. Her clothes took up too much space for that. Then again, maybe there was some home for rent she could live in. Her mind pictured Declan's A-frame. She would never imagine a home that shape would be appealing, but the inside of his home had been flooded with natural light and held a cozy vibe. Maybe her taste would change by the time she was ready to be a homeowner.

Jordan increased the volume of the car radio, singing at the top of her lungs as she drove toward Schermerhorn Trailhead. Apparently once they arrived there, the group would hike the Hideout Hollow Trail. She'd almost been giddy when Declan had texted her the information. That particular trail had an interesting history. Story had it that nine men formed the Slacker Gang with the intent of dodging the World War I draft. They'd hidden in the wilderness to live off the land. Years later, when that area had been established as a national park, the trail was named after them.

Pop had been the one to share the history behind the name when he and Mom had dragged Jordan and her siblings outside. The boys had thought the story nonsensical, and Pippen had been too young to care. But Jordan had found it fascinating, especially learning the gang members hadn't been successful and were still drafted. The memory had thoughts of her family swirling around her mind.

How she missed feeling like the dream team. All of the kids had been named after a basketball player. Pop said since Michael Jordan was the GOAT (greatest of all time), two of his children deserved to be named after him. Charles had been named after Charles Barkley and even had the same nickname he did: Chuck. Pippen had been a surprise years later. Pop claimed she was always meant to be named after Scottie Pippen, whether boy or girl. Apparently, mom thought Pippen more feminine, so they'd chosen that for her first name.

When Mom had passed, Jordan's siblings had clung together, becoming even more tight-knit, with Pop leading at the helm. But when Pop passed away at the hands of a drunk driver, they'd all scattered across Arkansas, barely keeping in touch. Jordan had tried to reach out to Pippen since they'd been living in the same city, but sometimes, she couldn't bring herself to dial Pip's number or come up with a text due to the overwhelming grief.

Then last Christmas, Michael had worked hard to bring them back together again. They'd gone to Starts and Stops for a gingerbread-making event and attended Christmas service together. He'd been so kind in offering a place for Jordan to live since she wouldn't have been able to afford rent in Fayetteville by herself.

She still couldn't believe her roommates had chosen Traun over Jordan. They'd asked her to move out of their group rental, the one that had all of their names listed. But since Jordan hadn't wanted to live the sinful life they'd proposed— three women sharing one man—she'd moved back home with Mike's welcome.

Now that Jordan was living back in Willow Springs, she prayed the family's togetherness would continue. She'd missed her brothers and sister desperately over the past year but had been unsure of how to reach across the divide.

Her thoughts refocused when she noticed her location. Turning into the parking lot, she threw the gear in Park. After grabbing her hiking-hair-don't-care cap and hiking pack, she exited the car. Her pack had been filled with protein bars and a couple of bottles of water before leaving home. Should be enough to keep her hydrated and satiated while out.

There was a group of people to her left. She scanned their faces, looking for Declan's. *Where was he?*

"Hey, Jordan."

She screamed, whirling around to find Declan right behind her. Her pulse drummed in her ears as her chest heaved from the force of her shriek.

A look of amusement crossed his face. "Scare easily, huh?"

"Only when someone sneaks up on me like some psycho in a horror movie." She shook her arms out, trying to will the heebie-jeebies away.

A soft chuckle escaped Declan's lips. "We're this way." He crooked a thumb over his shoulder.

"I'm ready." Now that her heart had settled into a normal rhythm, she was.

Only time would tell if Declan was ready for her evaluation. She would be taking a lot of mental notes and using her phone app for ones she absolutely didn't want to forget. Hopefully, he didn't stink as a guide, and coming up with a slogan would be a piece of cake. *God willing.*

Declan didn't know what surprised him more—Jordan flying in the air at his greeting or the fact that she owned decent hiking clothes. Before he'd even made his presence known, he'd stood there, gaping at her apparel. He'd recognized those boots in two seconds flat, only taking seconds more to catalog her pants and wicking T-shirt, and even noting where that ball cap came from.

Judging by a paint stain on her pants' cargo pocket, her clothing wasn't brand-new. No way she could've purchased hiking clothes that fancy when she'd asked to join the tour just a few hours ago. Online shipping wasn't that fast, and there was no hiking store in Willow Springs. Reasonable conclusion: she'd already owned the items.

The thought shook a few of his preconceived notions loose and left him wondering what else he'd misjudged about her. Then again, maybe she had the items from their high school years. Surely her parents had mandated outdoor fun. He knew his grandma had. His eyes scanned her figure again, noting other telltale signs of aging. Did that mean Jordan actually liked to hike?

Why is this bugging you so much?

It was a good question. Maybe because the thought of Jordan Wood, former varsity cheerleader, enjoying the outdoors enough to own hiking clothes shook him a little. How could a woman be that snooty if she was an adventurer? Mekayla certainly never would have willingly set foot outdoors unless it was to walk right back inside a place to shop.

Declan cleared his throat and reached for his hiking persona. Though he wouldn't call himself extroverted or even great with people, he did know how to make a hike fun and sound like he knew what he was talking about.

"All right, everybody. Now that we're all here, let me go over the rules. First, call me Declan. Not Dec, not Dee." He was still triggered after hearing Mekayla whine *Dec* after every argument.

"Second, if you feel like you're suffering from a medical emergency, don't be a hero, tell me. I can't help you if you decide to brave the day for the sake of a hike." He paused, meeting everyone's gaze to ensure they knew how sincere he was. "Trust me, the great outdoors will still be here when a doctor gives you the okay to return. Third, and this is important, do *not* wander from the group."

It was one reason he had people fill out liability forms prior to a guided tour. He didn't want someone's bad decision to get them seriously hurt—or to result in them casting the blame on him.

"Besides, if you do, you might hurt my feelings. Obviously, I'm not that great of a guide if you'd willingly walk away. Then again, this isn't meant to be a long-term relationship anyway."

A few people laughed. *Good.* Now he could stop trying to test the limits of his deodorant. Their previous blank stares had started to get under his skin.

"Last but not least, have fun. This is the Creator's backyard, and we have the chance to be more than a spectator. We can be a player on the field. I want to thank you for choosing Porter Adventures. Now, let's get to the adventure."

His gaze flicked to Jordan's. She nodded with approval and even wore a slight smile. He'd ignore the slight satisfaction that gave him. He didn't want the prom queen's approval.

Keep telling yourself that.

Declan motioned the group forward and prayed silently. *Lord God, please keep us safe today. I pray there are no injuries, no fainting spells, no mishaps of any kind. I pray the group has fun and remembers me when booking their next adventure.* He looked over his shoulder. *And I pray that Jordan finds the information she needs to help me improve my business.*

Wouldn't it be amazing if he could eventually hire another tour guide or even a secretary? Or accomplish his bigger dream of actually owning a storefront somewhere on Main Street? The building would be his home base, where tours could be booked right then and the items he used to encourage fun—tents, kayaks, etc.—could be stored somewhere other than where they currently resided in the shed in his backyard.

He took his time guiding the small group of five down the trail, pointing out the perfect backdrops for photos. One of the women brought a selfie stick with her, insisting they stop anytime they heard the sound of water. Apparently, she didn't heed the advice of not chasing waterfalls.

Declan mentally shook his head. Good thing no one could hear the thoughts running through his brain. He definitely had the dad jokes down. Maybe even an older generation's pop references. His grandma had listened to all kinds of music, and the lyrics had cemented themselves in his brain.

"Declan!" a voice called.

He turned, immediately scanning his hikers to make sure everyone looked well. The couple who had been hiking in the rear looked uneasy. The man had an arm up in the air to catch his attention.

Stopping the group, Declan began walking back toward them. "Everything okay?"

"Tina needs a snack break."

"Are you going to be sick?" he murmured,

making sure no one else could hear their conversation.

"No. Promise." Her eyes darted around, then met his once she was assured of their privacy. "I'm pregnant. I just need to eat before I get a little lightheaded."

Declan nodded. "Then snack time it is." He turned and raised his voice for the others to hear. "We're going to take a ten-to-fifteen-minute break. Now's the time to fuel up on those protein bars and drink some water. Don't guzzle."

Jordan walked up to him and tilted her head to the side. Her eyes squinted as if appraising him.

"What?" Heat climbed his neck.

"You're good at this."

"Why do you sound so surprised?" Should he feel offended? Because part of him had already jumped to the offense, ready to defend himself. He'd had to so many times with his ex-wife.

"Because your website leaves a lot to be desired. Yet you established your authority from the get-go." She held up a finger. "Made us laugh so we're comfortable in your presence." Another tick of the finger. "And not once have I been bored on this hike."

"Is my website really that bad?" He rubbed the back of his neck.

She nodded. "It really is, but thank goodness your guide skills are not." Her lips twitched as if she were hiding a smile.

The move didn't seem like her humor was directed *at* him. So he made sure to respond in a lighthearted manner, no matter what his twisted gut suggested. "Do you think you can help me?"

Her lips quirked up into a grin. "I know I can, Declan Porter. Just you watch. I've already made tons of notes." She held up her phone.

Once again, his insides quaked at the spark in her eyes. Only now he was recognizing it as a promise. He didn't have the heart to let Jordan know most people went back on their promises—his ex being number one. Trusting another woman wasn't the smartest thing to do. At least, Declan wouldn't do something ridiculous like trust Jordan Wood with his heart. That was safely guarded and would remain behind as many barriers as he could erect, no matter the pretty picture she painted.

Instead, he'd focus on the business relationship they were slowly establishing. If at any time, Jordan looked like she was going to cross the boundaries, he'd reestablish them with no problem. He laughed to himself. Yeah, as if a woman like Jordan would ever look at him in a romantic light. What was he worried about? Then again, he'd never imagined a varsity cheerleader/prom queen would enjoy the outdoors.

Declan cleared his throat. "Is this your first time hiking?"

She shook her head. "Why, do I look like a novice?"

"Uh, no." He slid his hands into his pockets. "Your clothing says you're experienced. Guess I just never thought you'd like nature."

She drew in an exaggerated inhale. "What's not to like? Arkansas is the prettiest place in the world."

Declan looked around at the landscape. He couldn't disagree.

"When our break is over, I'll drift to the back again. It's easier to take notes that way. Helps you forget I'm here."

He stifled the urge to snort. He still had eyes, didn't he? But she was kind of right. A few minutes into the hike, and he'd managed to block out her judging eyes. Not that he meant that in a negative light, but he'd been fully aware Jordan was grading his ability to be a tour guide so she could help him improve. Nothing like being put on display to make him want to crawl out of his skin and find someplace to hide.

At least the hike was halfway over. He dipped his head in acknowledgment to Jordan then roused the hikers. "Let's get back to fun."

Chapter Four

Did God think Jordan was a failure?

It was a question that went through her mind often, especially on a Sunday. Jordan sat straight back against the pew, careful not to move. Michael had taken the space to her right and Vivian, his girlfriend, to his left. Charles had come in late, so he ended up sitting a few rows behind.

Jordan wished coming to the Springs Bible Church didn't make her feel so inadequate. As her gaze shifted, taking in the others in the sanctuary, she couldn't help but note how many of them looked put together. Like they had everything figured out, and God was on their side.

Did He even pick sides?

Jordan blew out a breath.

"You okay?" Michael whispered, leaning toward her.

She nodded. Sharing her burdens in the middle of a sermon wasn't the right time or the right place.

He turned back to the pastor, so Jordan focused on appearing fine. Not that she was feeling horrible or anything. She just didn't understand what was expected of her. Michael wanted her to be a success and stop flitting from job to job. She got it. That made her appear unstable.

Charles—well, she wasn't really sure what Charles wanted. He seemed steeped in his own drama and too busy to peek and see that she was wallowing. And Pippen still had to figure out her own life, just like Jordan. Since Pippen was almost done with college and at an age when life still seemed a mystery, Jordan couldn't fault her.

But why couldn't Jordan have figured out the answers already?

Michael was only two years older but definitely leaps and bounds ahead of her. He had an established business that was in the black. Obviously, he'd managed to figure out the answers to life's questions. So why couldn't Jordan? Was having a career all she should aspire to? What about what God required of her? Christians were always talking about finding their purpose, but no one had sat down to explain what exactly that was. What *was* Jordan's purpose in the grand scheme of things?

Too bad receiving her bachelor's degree hadn't answered that question. Joining the workforce had been an easy thing to do since Pop owned the general store. But surely, narrowing her focus to merchandising wasn't the end of life's quest.

Pastor Liam ended the sermon with a prayer, then blessed them on their way out. Jordan rose along with everyone else in the congregation and followed her brother down the aisle toward the sanctuary exit. People she'd known all her life smiled in greeting while others stopped to say hello to her and her family. Jordan snuck around her brother as Cecily, one of Michael and Vivian's friends, stopped to talk to them.

Jordan didn't know why she was in such a funk, but maybe a cup of coffee and a pastry from the hospitality table would perk her up. She reached for a slice of banana bread just as a tiny hand jutted forward.

"River, be careful."

She turned at the sound of Declan's voice, then glanced at the little kid once more. With his face upturned and him munching on some bread, she noticed his features instead of the mop of curls. "Do you need a napkin?"

He stuffed another bite into his mouth, shaking his head.

Jordan chuckled softly.

"What did I tell you about stuffing your face?" Declan asked exasperatedly. He reached for a napkin and wiped his son's face.

"Morning, Declan."

He glanced up, froze, then blinked. "Jordan. Morning."

"I didn't see you in the sanctuary." She gestured over her shoulder. Her face heated. Of course he knew the direction. She reached for composure, hoping he wouldn't pick up on her embarrassment.

"I sit in the back. Makes for an easier exit to get River from Children's Church."

"Oh." She squeezed the clutch in her hand, searching for anything to make this less awkward.

Why was it so awkward? They'd hiked together yesterday—well, not together per se; there was a group of people, after all. Yet her brain now clamored for something to say. Perhaps uncovering a different layer of his personality had tied her tongue in knots.

"You were at our house yesterday," River announced, mouth now free of food.

"I was." She smiled down at River, then knelt before him. "Did you have fun at Children's Church?"

His head bobbed up and down. "We learned

about Noah's ark—" he threw his hands out "—and all the animals."

"That was always my favorite lesson. Did you play with the sock puppets?"

"Yes." River giggled. "I want to make one."

River was surprisingly easy to talk to. "Make sure to ask your dad. I'm sure he could help." She stood. "Well, I need to get home."

Declan opened his mouth, but Mike walked up just then.

"Declan and my man, River." He gave them each a fist bump, then looked at Jordan. "Vivian's coming over for lunch, if that's okay."

"Of course."

"Great." He grinned, brightening his countenance.

Vivian was so good for her brother. He'd been more than morose since Pop's death, but dating Vivian had seemed to pull him from the fog of grief.

"Hey." Mike looked at Declan. "You want to join us? There's plenty of food. Jordan here cooks enough for a whole army."

She rolled her eyes, but her insides tensed. Declan really wouldn't join them, would he? It was one thing to work together and another to share a meal.

"Uh, thanks, but we wouldn't want to intrude."

"No intrusion at all." Her brother slapped Declan on the back. "Like I said, we have plenty of food. The more the merrier."

Shame on those extroverts. But Jordan wouldn't say anything to stop Mike. He liked having people over, and even though she had a business relationship with Declan, she wouldn't mind spending more time with River. He was adorable. *But you don't need to insert yourself in their family life.*

Wouldn't that tempt her to enter the fray of a complicated life she was actively trying to avoid? She scoffed to herself. What was she thinking? It's not like she'd ever date Declan. She merely wanted to hang out with his son and see what entertaining words came out of his mouth. Plus, she'd cooked for other Willow Springs residents before with no problem. One lunch wasn't going to shake things up.

"Can we go, Dad?" River asked, not too quietly.

Declan's gaze dropped to his son, then shifted to Jordan's, a question filling his light blue eyes. She gave a slight nod, hoping Michael didn't read into the looks passing between them. Jordan didn't want to have to explain the exchange. He'd think something was up, even though there was nothing to investigate. She wasn't ready to tell her brother about her plan to improve Declan's business.

"Yes. Thank you for the invite," Declan said.

"Anytime, man."

Jordan kept her face neutral and gave a little wave to River. "See you at the house."

"See ya," River exclaimed cheerfully.

Jordan followed Mike out of the church and spared him a glance. "Anyone else you want to invite while you're at it?"

"What? What's the big deal?"

"What if I just wanted our family there?" When she'd texted Chuck this morning to see if he was coming to church, she'd invited him over for lunch afterward. It seemed like it had been a minute since only the three of them had dined together.

"Declan's church family," her brother said.

Sometimes he seemed so clueless. *Ugh.* "That's not what I meant, and you know it."

Mike rested a hand on the cab of his truck. "You know Mom and Pop were all about hospitality. Shouldn't we carry on that legacy as well?"

She wasn't trying to be inhospitable. But she and Mike did share a living space. He couldn't just go inviting people over all willy-nilly. She explained that.

Mike sighed. "Sorry. I'll be more aware. Just

remember what Mom always said about entertaining people."

"If you insinuate Declan is an angel, I might lose it." Jordan clenched her jaw. Whether from the ache of not having her parents around or the thought of being nicer to Declan, she couldn't quite tell.

Mike threw his head back and laughed.

Jordan rolled her eyes and shoved him lightly. "You're a pain."

He swung an arm around her shoulder. "You love me. I'm the best big brother ever."

"You wish."

"You mean to tell me you have a better one?"

"You're my only big brother."

His brows raised. "So then, you agree?"

"By default." She smirked at him.

"Fine." Mike laughed. "I'll take it."

Jordan shook her head, then rounded the back toward the passenger side of the truck. Mike was loveable, even if he had the overwhelming need to fill their house with people. Wasn't running a general store and renting tiny homes enough for him? Then again, it might be the change that Vivian had wrought in his life.

Jordan couldn't fault him for that. Only the thought of Declan in her own domain, so closely after being in his, made her a little uneasy. Going on a hike was simple enough. No

one was in the other's space and kept proverbial bloodshed from ensuing. Plus, Jordan had
maintained a little distance from the rest of the
hikers since she'd been there for a job.

A slow smile lifted her lips. Maybe she could
turn lunch into another business consultant
meeting. One where she showed Declan the pre-
liminary ideas she'd come up with for giving his
website a face-lift. Surely that would be enough
to firmly establish the lines between them and
keep them in the safety zone. No need to get
close to another man unless it was of a professional nature.

What had he done?

With one glance from his squishy-cheeked
son, Declan had caved faster than a sinkhole
in Florida. Now he found himself trudging up
the steps behind Jordan and her brother. River
happily chattered, not really talking to anyone,
just making noise to be heard. The only time
his son was quiet was while sleeping. Other-
wise, the boy was the very definition of activity.

"Can I help y'all with anything?" Declan
asked once on the main floor of the Woods'
living quarters.

He discreetly looked around the open space.
In all his years living in Willow Springs, Declan had never been above the general store.

Yes, he'd gone to high school with Mike, Jordan and Chuck, but they'd never really been friends. Though he and Jordan were in the same grade, Mike had been two grades above them, with Chuck two years behind. Of course, Declan had never really had many friends—one or two here and there. The Wood siblings had always been just acquaintances, so seeing their home felt a little surreal.

Their place held a relaxed atmosphere, and photos of the entire family were scattered throughout their space. There was one picture on the end table, another above some bookshelves and more on a wall that looked like the beginning of a hallway. He even noticed a picture of Mr. Wood.

Declan swallowed, thinking of the loss they'd suffered when their father had passed two years ago. Well, almost two years. Did their loss feel fresh, or had they begun to find pockets of peace in the midst of it all?

"I've got everything all ready since I used a pressure cooker," Jordan stated. "Or the slow cooker function on it anyway."

He nodded, not even sure what kind of appliance that was. How did it have more than one function? Declan used the stove, microwave and oven, and that was it. Well, also a fire pit when camping.

"River, do you want to play with some toys?" Jordan asked.

"Oh, no. He's okay," Declan interjected.

"But I *do* want to play with toys, Dad." River's brown eyes seemed to grow twice in size as his mouth turned downward in a plea of understanding.

"It's just an old train set," Jordan stated.

"How old?" he asked cautiously. No need to ruin a family heirloom.

Mike laughed. "Not an antique, man. He won't mess anything up, promise."

"Okay. Thank you." Declan nodded at his son.

"Yes!" River threw a hand up, then rushed toward Jordan.

She opened the ottoman in front of the sectional and pulled out a locomotive, caboose and some other cars. River immediately bent down and started hitching them together. While River was preoccupied, Jordan walked into the kitchen, so Declan followed behind.

"Thank you for that."

"Sure." Her lips curved upward. "I hear kids don't like to be bored."

Understatement of the decade. Whenever River acted up, Declan would have his son sit down for five minutes. Just that simple act was enough for the boy to slide further into a meltdown. Now they were finally at the stage where River understood it would be better to be still so Declan wouldn't continue adding minutes for every time River tried to get up early.

"The only times he's bored is in the car and right before he falls asleep."

Jordan cracked a smile. "He seems like an energetic guy."

That was the truth.

"Hey, I had a thought." She tilted her head, studying him. "Maybe after lunch, I could show you my ideas for your website."

He jerked back. She had plans already? "Really? Wow, I wasn't expecting that so fast. That sounds good."

"That might have been the most I've ever heard you say at once." Jordan tilted her head to the side, eyes studying him.

It took everything within him not to fidget under her stare. "When I'm comfortable, I can talk a lot. Promise." Not that he was making a specific promise to her. Wasn't that just an expression?

"Does our home make you uncomfortable?"

You make me uncomfortable. At least he had the sense to keep those words to himself. "No. It's nice."

"Thanks. Your excessive flattery is making my cheeks turn red."

Declan chuckled. "We're kind of strangers, Jordan. Sorry if my brain can't think of a conversation starter."

"Well, good thing I know how to talk. What did you think of the sermon?"

Pastor Liam always had a good word to share on Sundays. But Declan didn't think that was what Jordan would want to hear.

"Come on, Declan. Say something. Pretend we're on a hike and it's just wide-open spaces."

And now he was thinking about that one country song. *Focus.* "All right. I think Pastor Liam always knows how to get me thinking about my walk with God. I haven't been to a Sunday service yet where I don't walk out talking to God and asking Him to examine me."

Her mouth dropped open. *Good.* He had stunned her. "What about you? How did you like it?" Let her get a taste of her own medicine.

Not that he was trying to be vindictive. He'd thought they'd reached an understanding after the hike yesterday, but she seemed to be eyeing him under a microscope even more. Was it because he confused her or something else?

"Wait, wait, wait a minute." She waved her hand in the air. "You ask God to examine you? For what?"

"Usually in a way that's related to the sermon. For instance, today Pastor Liam talked about perfect peace. I asked God if there were areas where I wasn't at peace."

Jordan propped her chin on her hand, gaze intense. "Did He answer?" she asked quietly.

"Not yet."

"But you believe He will?"

"He always does." Declan slid his hands into his pockets, trying to keep from fidgeting. He didn't know how to interact with this new Jordan—the one who seemed genuinely curious about the nature of Declan's faith. What alternate universe had he stepped into?

She bit her lip. "I'm not sure I'm brave enough to ask Him that."

"Then how can you get closer to Him?" Declan rested his hands on the countertop. He took a deep breath. "God's not a punishing God, Jordan. If there were any flaws in you, He'd point them out in the same way a dad points out something in his children."

Jordan shook her head. "Pop about blew a gasket when I snuck back in the house after sneaking out to break curfew."

Declan laughed. "I imagine he did. But I bet you don't recall him yelling when you were really young. Maybe even River's age."

A thoughtful expression crossed her face. "I don't."

"Good." Declan shifted his stance. "That's

how I imagine God deals with us. With patience, because He knows we're not at His level. I don't yell at River because there's no point. He's five. But I probably would blow a gasket if he was older. Remember, though, earthly dads aren't perfect like our Heavenly Father."

"Okay," she said. "I'll remember. Maybe one day I'll try that."

He nodded, not sure what else to say.

A knock sounded on the door and Michael opened it, letting Vivian in.

"Now we eat!" Jordan called out.

Lunch went by relatively painlessly. Gratitude filled Declan as Mike and Jordan kept the conversation going. Even River chimed in, always with a comment that had all the adults laughing. Soon they finished their meal, and River went back to playing with the trains while Michael and Vivian cleaned up.

That left Declan and Jordan at the dining table to talk business. She grabbed her notes and opened her laptop to show him a mockup site.

She pointed to the screen. "This company offers free website layouts, but you have to do all the customization yourself. I found a theme I thought fit your business, so now I'm messing around with a few things to see how I can tailor it to Porter Adventures." She snapped her fingers. "I also have some logo ideas."

Jordan opened her notebook, flipped a few pages, then slid the book toward him. "These three are my top contenders. What do you think?"

Declan studied the circular logos. One had the outline of Arkansas in the middle and a man wearing a hiking pack. A walking stick was in the center, and the words "Porter Adventures" were arched above the figure. Below it in a reverse arc read, "Let's have an adventure."

"Wow, Jordan, this is amazing. I really like the slogan." It felt like him. He thought she'd make him sound stuffy and unrealistic. Maybe she saw more than he'd realized.

Her grinned widened. "Yay. What about the logos? Any one of them stick out to you?"

"Um, I only looked at the first. Just a sec." He scanned the other two. They were similar in nature, except one was missing the Arkansas shape. Instead, a river went through the circle and a man kayaked in the middle. The last one incorporated all three but seemed busy.

"I like the first one the best."

"Great. I'll do some different color options to it next. Do you think your supplier could add the logo to the gear we'll be selling in the store?"

That was an excellent question. "I'll find out."

"We're off to a great start." She closed her laptop. "I want to meet up tomorrow if possible and talk about the different types of tours you offer."

That didn't sound terrible. "Okay. I'll text you once I look at my schedule."

"You don't have it on your phone?"

He shook his head. "My phone is pretty basic."

"But all phones these days have a calendar." She held out a hand. "Pass it over and I'll help you out. It'll be better to have it in your phone, especially when someone wants to schedule a tour on the fly. You don't want to have to wait till you get back to your house and have access to your laptop."

Declan unlocked his phone and passed it over. She sent a look his way—one that implied, *You're hopeless* and *What am I going to do with you?* Funny how the second one echoed his thoughts exactly, because as Jordan walked him through syncing his calendars, a spark of awareness shot through him and scrambled his senses. It was something that made him want to grab River and run to the safety of his home.

Surely Jordan would never look at him with interest. She seemed to like the single life; at least, he'd never heard of her bringing a guy to Willow Springs to meet her family. Not to mention, Declan would never make the same mistakes he did with Mekayla. He couldn't date a woman solely based on attraction.

Not that Jordan was giving him any inclination that she found him good-looking. She was simply helping him, and he would treat her with the professional respect she deserved. Besides, she talked more to River than him. Her no-nonsense demeanor was clearly a sign for Declan to stay in his lane.

He blew out a breath. *You're safe from future heartache. Relax, it's just a business meeting.*

Chapter Five

Since Michael was working on the tiny homes, Jordan had the use of his office. Declan had dropped by so they could map out a plan to overhaul Porter Adventures and bring him more customers. Right now, Jordan was trying to understand why Declan offered such limited tours.

"So, wait. You don't offer any team-building outings? No overnight camping trips?" Jordan tried to tone down the incredulity in her voice—she could hear it plain as day—but the shake of Declan's head just didn't compute. She sputtered for a few more seconds.

Lord, I don't want to insult him, but this seems so ludicrous to me. Season my words so that I can offer a beneficial alternative. "All right. I would strongly suggest changing that."

He nodded slowly. "Why's that? Do you not think I can get more business as is?"

Nope. But an empathetic answer wouldn't help any. "Maintaining the status quo won't make you more competitive. You definitely need to enter a higher competition range. Adding different tour packages would help in the long run."

He rubbed his chin. "Okay, I can see that."

Phew. "Do any of those sound viable?" She snapped her fingers. "What about kayaking? You could have kayaks for people to rent or just take them on river tours."

A light lit his eyes. "That would actually be kind of great. Since I don't have a storefront, renting them out probably isn't a good idea. However, I could definitely take them on tours. Maybe store a couple of kayaks in my shed with everything else."

Jordan tapped her pen against her chin. "What if we could free up some space at the general store for you to rent the kayaks?"

"How?" He leaned forward.

"Well, I'd have to double check with Michael, but maybe we can display them on the front porch with a rental sign. Have whatever paperwork you'd need people to sign and then rent them at the rate you feel is best. We could add a clause to the contract specifically for the kayaks and not charge more for doing so." Maybe it would make the lulls at the general store less

frequent if people were coming in to rent outdoor equipment.

A huge grin split Declan's face, and goose
bumps pebbled her skin. What an odd reaction.
Just ignore it, Jay. Probably a draft.

"That sounds perfect," Declan said. "Maybe
I can even get my logo added to the kayaks."

"Yes. That's a must." She slid a folder over to
him. "This is a list of all the businesses in Arkansas that advertise outdoor adventures like
you. I've got a spreadsheet of their price points,
the packages they offer, etcetera. I wanted you
to see the data for yourself."

He waved a hand in the air. "I never thought
you'd cheat me. You don't have to go through
all that trouble."

She blinked. *What to say to that?* It seemed
like everyone in her life, at one time or another,
doubted the words coming out of her mouth. For
someone—a man at that—to take her for her
word left her actually floundering and speechless. "Um. Thanks."

Jordan cleared her throat, trying to regroup.
"I made a list of the ideas I think you should incorporate and the future benefits I believe it'll
bring to your company. Everything's in this
folder." She patted the object in discussion.
"How 'bout you look it over and tell me what
I can do to get those changes implemented?"

Declan rubbed his short blond beard and sighed. "I'm not trying to be difficult. But I am a single father. I can't do guided tours any time of day."

"Understandable. Have you ever thought of hiring another person?"

He smirked.

"Right. Not enough money." Her nails clicked against the tabletop. "Okay. What if you make an arrangement with a babysitter who can do overnight stays? Maybe have her guarantee the days she can sit for River and be willing to be on call, sometimes short notice."

"What do you mean?"

"I mean, if she can always do Fridays because she has kids and never goes anywhere on Fridays, then that means you can advertise Friday-only camping trips on your website. That way people know you're not going out on just any ol' day."

"That actually makes sense."

She rolled her eyes. "Imagine that." She let out a light laugh to let him know she was joking. Why did Jordan always feel like she was waiting for life to kick her when she was already down?

Not that she was. Being back home had actually alleviated a lot of stress. But being around Declan made her think of her ex. Not that Declan and Traun were *anything* alike. But the little flutters that erupted inside her when Declan was near made her remember how she felt the same excitement when she first started dating her ex. Only now the memories were doused by the shock and betrayal of his actions. If she could get giddy over Declan despite knowing how badly her last relationship had failed, was she doomed to repeat her mistakes?

"Okay," Declan said, interrupting her musings. "I'll see if I can get some guaranteed days from a sitter."

Right. *Stick to business.* "Great. Please really consider adding the team-building outings. You could offer day trips or even mini retreats." His steady stare that showed he was listening loosened her words. "Think about it—if it's a small company, they could rent some of the tiny homes and stay for two or three days. You'll take them out during the day. They can come back to Simplicity for the evening, maybe even take the time to explore Willow Springs. Then get back out into nature the next day."

"Do you have an idea of what the other companies are doing for team-building exercises?"

She tapped the folder and Declan's eyes widened.

"Information overload?" she asked. Maybe she had packed too much into one meeting for him. She didn't want to inundate future clients, so if this was too much, she may need to temper her initial assessment going forward.

"Uh..." His Adam's apple bobbed.

Yep, she'd overwhelmed him. She slid the folder back toward herself. "Let me make this easier. Tell me what you want to know, and I'll just give you the information."

Declan's shoulders relaxed a fraction. "Uh, okay. What's the average price for a kayaking trip?"

That she could answer without rifling through the numerous papers she'd printed out. "If they want to rent them, around seventy-five. If they want a guide, you can add fifty to a hundred more dollars."

Declan's eyes bugged out.

Jordan had to stifle a laugh. "Yep. About double your pricing."

"That's ridiculous." Disbelief tinged his tone, but the hope in his eyes told her a different story.

"I think if you overhaul your website and add a few more adventure packages, you'll realize that requesting more money is feasible. You have a great way with people. Don't let your hesitancy keep you from what you're worth." Did that sound like a good pep talk, or was she only helping herself?

Declan groaned, sliding his head into his hands. Jordan fought the urge to pat him on the back. She was grateful the desk was keeping the distance between them. Jordan didn't want her guard to be inadvertently lowered and start feeling any vibes toward him other than those of a natural working relationship.

She swallowed. "The good news is we can turn this around."

"Are you sure?" He lowered his hands while blowing out a huff of air.

"Positive. Once you decide on everything, we'll get the website up and running with the new pricing and all the treks you'll offer."

"All right. Thanks, Jordan." He stood. "I'll text you once I've got it all figured out."

"Or email me if you have a lot to say." She almost wanted to laugh at the thought.

Declan Porter was like a closed box. Had he been that way in high school? She couldn't recall from that one class they'd had together. Was he just extremely introverted? For some reason, the thought made her wince. She'd never gone out of her way to make him feel comfortable, but if she had…

He shifted, drawing her attention back to him and away from memory lane.

A smirk curved his lips. "How about a voice text?"

"Whatever works for you, man of many words."

He shook his head. "Have a good day, Jordan."

"You too." She stood to follow him, then snapped her fingers. "Oh, I almost forgot. I have something for River." She turned back to the desk and grabbed the little brown gift bag.

Mike had terrible gift-bag choices—something else she wanted to change—so the nondescript paper bag was all she'd had to put River's surprise in.

Declan's eyebrows rose. "What is it?"

"The triceratops plush for River. I remember him saying he didn't have it, so I got one for him."

Declan's jaw tightened. "Why?"

Jordan straightened, wary of his tone. *Had she done something wrong?* "I was only trying to be nice."

He studied her, blue eyes looking ice cold when they had been so warm moments before. Not that she'd *really* noticed. Just a basic observation.

"Then thank you." He took the bag, dipped his head and ducked out of the room.

Jordan stared as his figure disappeared from view. She really had no idea what to think of Declan. The quiet that cloaked him had to be a defense mechanism, right? No one was *that* quiet just because.

He did come alive outdoors though. Maybe he was only quiet when uncomfortable. And why did the thought of him being uncomfortable around her tweak something in her middle?

Growing up with Chuck and Pop had shown her guys who were on the quiet side. She and Michael, on the other hand, could mingle with the best of them…for about an hour, two hours max. Then they needed some quiet place to decompress.

Thinking about her family was only a cover. Jordan desperately wanted to figure out Declan Porter, despite the fact she had no clue why she wanted to.

Declan walked through the French doors to his back deck and sat in one of the two brown Adirondack chairs. With River finally asleep, the day's events came flooding to mind at once. Declan took a sip from his bottled water and let out a sigh.

Jordan had hit him with a bunch of information this morning. Although he'd been a little swamped by the details, humiliation had become the leading emotion.

When he'd moved back to Willow Springs, Declan had needed a new job in the area. Moving his outdoor guide business to Willow Springs had seemed like a no-brainer. Thanks to Mekayla, he'd been able to start the company with the money she'd given him before deciding she no longer wanted to be a wife or mother. And before she decided that money was actually a loan and not a gift—though he had a feeling her new husband was behind the push to get the funds back.

His basic website had only needed one change—the location of where he gave tours. But not once had Declan thought to update his site. Was that something companies did often? Why hadn't he figured that out sooner? Times changed, so why wouldn't websites change as well?

He shook his head as he stared up at the night sky. As much as he wanted to wallow in pity, it wouldn't do much good. His grandma had always said there was no use crying over spilled milk when a paper towel would get rid of the mess right quick. He only wished the paper towel would act as currency and pull him onto better financial footing. At least he'd been able to make some decisions regarding the options Jordan had given him.

Lord, it seems like I'm always one step behind. Will I ever be on equal footing with my peers?

Comparison's a sin, Declan Porter. Don't go trying to be a lion when God made you to be a lamb.

He winced at the echo of his grandma's words. Declan knew better than to argue with his grandma, but he'd always thought, *I want to be a lion*. They were fierce loners but ran a pride. What he knew about lambs was less than that. He only knew they didn't appear to be scaring off any predators.

Maybe now was the time to accept his fate. He was a lamb, living a docile existence. He'd probably do best to start searching for a backup job. Based off all the information Jordan had shared with him this morning, Declan wasn't cut out to do this long term. It was a wonder he'd managed till now.

If he could have another job waiting on the sidelines, the transition from business owner to employee would be a lot easier to swallow.

His phone chimed, pulling him out of his self-pitying thoughts. A quick look at his device showed a text message waiting from Jordan.

Jordan: Thanks for sending me the email. I just have a few follow-up questions.

Did she ever rest? Declan typed a reply.

Declan: Go ahead.

Jordan: What's the max amount of people you can take on a hiking tour or a team-building tour?

Declan: 5

Jordan: What if you had an assistant with you?

Declan raised an eyebrow.

Declan: Why? You volunteering?

Jordan: Only if Michael could spare me.

Though he'd seen her hike with his own two eyes, Declan couldn't imagine Jordan fishing or roughing it in nature. The thought drew a genuine chuckle from him as he tried to imagine her in waders or cleaning fish. The thought seemed so far-fetched. Not because he didn't think her capable, but Jordan seemed so…girly. Or maybe the slight attraction he felt was being masked by his assumption that she'd rather be shopping or exploring the world of fashion.

Jordan messaged a few more questions that he answered. Finally, she thanked him for doing business so late in the evening.

Declan: Are you finally calling it a night?

His phone rang. *Great.* He'd somehow invited an actual vocal conversation. "Hello?"

"It's only eight, Declan. Don't tell me you're off to sleep."

He smirked. "No, but I have stopped working for the day." Unlike the woman on the line with him.

"So have I. This is my secondary job. The one that doesn't yet pay the bills."

"Yet, huh? You seem confident." Wasn't that the part that drew him in—no, piqued his interest in a friendly way?

"Hey, I promised you I would turn your business around. I keep my promises, Declan Porter." She huffed, and he thought he heard her mumble, "Unlike some people."

Declan was curious enough and bold enough—*Thank you, phones, for helping me avoid looking her in the eye*—to ask, "Who's let you down?"

"What?" Surprise coated her voice.

"You said, 'Unlike some people,' didn't you?"

"I didn't realize I said that out loud." She sounded shocked.

Should he leave it alone? Not tug on the string dangling in front of him like a carrot? Telling himself he needed to know who he was doing business with, Declan continued the conversation. "Well now, inquiring minds want to know who you're talking about." Had she experienced a major disappointment or the normal kind?

He'd actually be surprised if she'd suffered a huge letdown. She seemed too upbeat. Then again, not everyone gave in to the urge to retreat like he had.

"I didn't know you could be this chatty, Declan Porter."

"Anyone can talk openly on the phone. You don't have to face the person you're speaking to." He winced. Why'd he say that out loud?

Jordan laughed. "Just for that, I'll video-chat with you next time."

He shuddered. "Please don't."

She laughed again, and just like in person, she didn't hold back. Warmth filled him at the sound, and his lips twitched in response.

He needed to get this conversation back on track. "Hey now, don't think I've forgotten about the question. Who's disappointed you, Jordan Wood?"

"Don't we disappoint one another from time to time? Humans are so fallible."

"Ain't that the truth?" He grimaced.

"Sounds like you have your own story to tell."

Declan snorted. "Don't we all have stories to share? I mean, humans are so very..." He laughed. "Yeah, I got nothing. Didn't want to repeat your word."

"I get it. Wittiness is not a trait you possess."

"Ouch, but true." It was almost nice talking

to another person over the age of five. Though River could definitely hold his own in a conversation, Declan appreciated the back-and-forth communication with Jordan. River liked to hog airtime.

"Well, good night, Mr. Porter. I'll get these changes added to the website and press Publish tomorrow."

He gulped. "Already?"

"You didn't think I was going to wait for your birthday, did you?"

Wouldn't that be ideal? Only that would prevent the bank from considering Porter Adventures for a small business loan. "My birthday was in February, so we'd be waiting a while."

"Oh, we don't want to wait another eleven months. Anyhoo, good night, Porter."

"Night, Jordan."

Declan set the phone on his table and stared out into the woods. He could tell himself he didn't care that Jordan hadn't opened up to him, but that would be a lie if the disappointment rolling through him was any indication.

Besides, women couldn't be trusted, right? Hadn't the whole fiasco with Mekayla taught him that? One minute he'd pledged his love and devotion, the next he'd been left in a one-bedroom apartment with a one year old who didn't understand why his mother was suddenly gone.

Had he been insensitive to Mekayla's needs? Had she suffered from postpartum depression and he missed the signs? Though part of him believed she would've told him if she had been experiencing that. The only clue he'd had that she'd been unhappy was the note she left saying she had to go find herself.

A year later, he'd received divorce papers with a note saying marriage wasn't for her. Which was why discovering she'd married once more had come as such a shock. It just didn't track.

Not that staring out into the void would give him the answers he was searching for. Declan had to accept the fact he may never know why he hadn't been enough. But until he could figure out how to be a husband a woman would want to stay with till death, Declan would pour all his love and attention on the son he'd been blessed to raise. God willing, River would never doubt his worth or feel the stings of Mekayla's abandonment like he had.

And despite the not-so-warm feelings toward Mekayla, Declan would do his best to keep the line of communication open so that River could have a relationship with his mom. A relationship Declan had never experienced. Not that he wasn't thankful his grandma had taken care of him, but feeling that loss of a mother, he never wanted River to feel the same hurt.

Sadly, though, Mekayla hadn't used her visitation rights, only asked for the start-up money.

And if Declan worked himself to the ground to get it, he would. Anything to make sure she had an avenue back to River.

Chapter Six

Pippen was here!

Jordan squeezed her little sister tightly and then pulled back to take a good look at her. "You always look so pretty."

The hue in Pippen's cheeks darkened. At twenty-two, Jordan's little sister seemed to have that youthful glow in her brown skin. Her black hair had been contorted into a single braid that wrapped around her head like a halo, emphasizing the fresh, innocent look.

"So do you, sis. Are you enjoying living in Willow Springs as a grown-up?" Pippen asked.

"I am." Being known by her fellow Willow Springs residents was a balm to Jordan's soul. It gave her time and space to heal from her ex's betrayal and that of her ex-friends.

She cleared her throat. "Of course I'd have a better time if Mike would let me make some changes around here."

As far as Jordan was concerned, agreeing to let Declan have shelf space didn't count. Why was Michael so willing to let Declan sell his gear out of the shop and suggest where to shelve it all and not give Jordan any other leeway in the store? Wasn't she supposed to be running it in her brother's stead?

Pippen gave her the side-eye. "Like what?"

"I have some ideas for changing the layout of the store, adding some different items and whatnot." She even had some sketches created with her ideas in mind. Not that she was the best artist, but the drawings served their purpose.

"Humph. People always trying to fix things that aren't broken."

Ugh. Jordan thought Pippen would be on her side. So much for getting her and Chuck to talk to Mike for her. "Just because something's not broken doesn't mean it can't be improved."

"Mike runs things, Jay. That's the way it's always been and always will be." Pippen gave her an exasperated look.

But what if it wasn't? Jordan straightened. "Speaking of the store, I need to go open for the afternoon shift." She set her salad bowl in the sink. "Lunchtime is over."

"Remember how Mom always said, 'Don't leave your dirty dish in the sink'?" Wistfulness filled Pippen's jet-black eyes.

Jordan smiled softly. "I do. But I'll clean it when I get back. I don't have enough time since I had a late lunch."

"Sure, sure." Pippen blinked, as if snapping back to reality.

"How long will you be home?" It seemed like forever since she'd seen Pippen, even though they'd seen each other at Christmas.

Still, three months was a long time when she was used to being able to see her so easily in Fayetteville.

Pippen tugged her suitcase from around the sofa and toward the hall that led to the bedrooms. "Just for the week. I'll return Sunday in order to prep for Monday's classes."

"Wanna do something while you're here? Girls' day or night out?" Jordan could use some sister time.

"Of course, Jay. I won't desert you."

Jordan kissed her sister on the cheek, then headed for the door. "See you later." She walked out of the room and down the stairs toward the general store.

Declan would be here soon with the first shipment of goods he wanted to sell in the store. They were coming in three parts because his distributor had to put the new logo onto the items. Jordan couldn't wait to see how they turned out. The quickening in her pulse at the thought of seeing Declan meant nothing.

It was just that the phone call they'd had seemed to break down preconceived notions and give her a better glimpse of who Declan Porter really was. Seeing that vulnerable side of him had prompted Jordan to examine herself and figure out why she had trouble opening up to others. Was that why her ex, Traun, had decided to date her roommates instead?

Her thoughts were interrupted by the bell chiming over the front door. Jordan waved to the customers walking in. After scanning their items and making small talk, they walked out of the front door a moment before Declan came in.

Jordan swallowed. She couldn't help but view Declan through new eyes, *curious* eyes. Then she noticed the box he carried and scooted around the counter to offer aid.

"Do you need help?"

"Nah. I've got two more to bring inside though. I'll be back. River is in the car waiting impatiently to get out of his car seat."

Jordan checked her watch. "Why isn't he in school?"

"Early dismissal."

"Want me to get him?" She didn't know why, but River didn't make her uneasy like other children did. Usually, she clammed up around them, never knowing what to say or do around the kids. But River put Jordan at ease. He always had discussion points on the tip of his tongue for the ready listener.

"Really?" Declan froze mid-step.

"Sure."

"Thank you."

She nodded and followed him outside. Was it bad she would've known which Jeep was his even if there'd been more than one? Swatting the thought away, Jordan opened the back door and smiled at a grinning River.

"Hey there."

He waved. "Hi, Ms. Jordan."

"Your dad said I could help you out of your seat."

"I can do it myself." River pressed the red button and removed the straps from his chest. "Dad told me to wait so I would be safe."

Jordan helped him hop out of the vehicle. "I'm glad you listened. Safety is important."

"That's what Dad says." His curls ruffled in the wind.

She wanted to scoop him up and plant kisses all over his squishy cheeks. Instead, she held out a hand and led him across the parking lot.

"Thank you."

"You're welcome, River."

"And thank you for Nelson."

"Who?" She could feel her eyebrows head for her hairline.

"My tri'tops. Dad gave him to me and said you got it."

"Oh, you're welcome." Her cheeks heated at the scrutiny from the five-year-old. Why did his steady gaze make her feel embarrassed?

"Do you watch *Dino Treks*?" River asked as they walked inside.

"No. What's that?"

"It's a YouTube show. They dig for fossils."

"That sounds amazing."

He nodded vigorously. "When I grow up, I'm going to save dinosaurs from extinction."

Jordan bit her lip. The earnest expression in his eyes had her heart doing flips and her mouth remaining mute.

"Where should this stuff go?" Declan asked, huffing from the exertion of lifting the last two boxes.

What was in them? Her mind went blank as she struggled to recall what items were being added to their inventory today. She pointed toward the empty shelving near the checkout counter. "I cleared space for you after my shift last night. Will this be enough room?" Michael had seemed to think so, but Jordan was a little skeptical.

Declan examined the space in question. "I

think so." He turned toward her. "Oh, and the kayaks are supposed to come by the end of the week. I already received the display rack for them. The vinyl stickers of the logo I ordered should be here soon. I'll also email you the wording I'd like for the rental agreement."

Jordan nodded. "Sounds good." Things were moving right along.

His lips quirked. "Thanks." Declan pulled a multitool from his belt loop and cut open the box.

"I could have given you a box cutter." Jordan had become accustomed to using it to unpack the general store's inventory to ensure all her digits were kept safe.

"You do know I'm an outdoor guide, right?" He grinned in her direction.

She blinked, momentarily stunned by his display of humor. *And not at all by his rugged looks.*

"Us guides know how to use a multitool. It's from our outdoor 101 class," Declan continued.

"Well, of course you took a class."

His low laugh filled the store. Jordan turned away and started stocking the shelves with the miniature first aid kits. She paused to study his new logo. The blue background worked great with the gray hiker and the slogan written in orange. Simple yet effective.

"Besides the kits, what else did you bring?" she asked.

"Hiking packs and multitools."

"All with your logo?" River handed her another first aid kit, brimming with delight.

She could only imagine how important he felt helping them. She mouthed a thank-you and continued lining the shelves. "When do the hiking boots and rain gear come in?"

"I'd have to check my emails." Declan opened the last box. "When I get home, I'll be sure to send you a copy of all the delivery dates so we can set up times for me to bring the rest of the stuff in. I don't want to disturb your routine."

"I appreciate that." Why did his simple consideration make her eyes feel a little watery?

She shook off her thoughts, focusing on the task at hand. Maybe by the next shipment, Jordan could convince Mike to rearrange the store or something. Some items weren't selling, and were merely taking up valuable room in the store. Declan deserved more retail space if his products cleared the shelves.

How could she show Mike that her proposed changes weren't going to ruin Pop's legacy but only enhance it? *Patience, Jay.*

Easier said than done, but something she needed to practice regardless. She had to prepare herself in case Mike wouldn't heed her advice, even if she helped Declan improve his business. Maybe then she'd take a chance and go into business on her own.

But immediately at the thought, her stomach tensed. She didn't want to work on her own, despite the fun she'd had toiling for Declan's business. Continuing to work in the family general store gave her a purpose. Allowed her to give back to the legacy Pop and Mom had built for their family. It was one reason she hadn't bothered trying to find a job anywhere else. Being here filled her with memories and made her feel useful. It had been so long since she'd felt that way. Plus, she wanted to make her family proud.

By the time they'd stocked everything, River was happily chatting about "tri'tops" and what made them the coolest herbivores. When he took a moment to breathe, Declan stepped forward, laying a hand on his son's shoulder.

"I've already gotten requests for tours since the website went live." Declan's cheeks pinked. Was he embarrassed, or was it something else?

Before Jordan could speculate and investigate using subtle tactics—friendly conversation for the win—Declan continued speaking. "Thank you."

"Of course. Do the guide inquiries all fit into your schedule?"

He nodded. "I made sure they would. Knowing what days I can have a babysitter no matter what really helped me."

River looked up, pointing to plush animals. "Can I, Dad?"

"Sure."

Jordan was glad a standby babysitter would work out for them. Even though Declan might say she'd been winging ideas, Jordan had been poring over her old textbooks and online notes. Anything to guide her so that she could help Declan become a success. *Please Lord, help us. I want a purpose.*

Maybe helping struggling businesses could be that if Mike decided she wasn't cut out for the family store. Not that she thought he'd lean that way, but some days she didn't know what to think about her big brother as her boss.

Jordan took a step forward so River wouldn't hear her and lowered her tone. "You look like something's on your mind."

Declan ran a hand over his chin. "I'm actually waiting to hear from the local bank. I asked for a loan, but they need proof my business will be viable."

Jordan schooled her features. She had no idea that Declan was in such dire straits. But wait... "What's the loan for?"

"I need to pay off someone."

"Oh. So it's not a loan for the business?"

He shook his head. "I have a meeting with the loan officer next week, and he will want financial information on my business." Declan swallowed. "It would be really great if you could convince patrons to buy the items here." He gestured to the shelves.

He didn't say how much the loan meant to him, but judging by his body language, this was huge. "I'll do my best." She bit her lip.

God willing, they'd get some of their renters to add the items to their carts. "You know, maybe I can start a newsletter with a new-items feature or something."

Declan's blue eyes widened. "That would be great. Other stores do it, so why not the general store?"

Why not, indeed? Maybe Mike wouldn't be so opposed to this idea. Would it be terrible if she asked Declan to bring up the idea to her brother? *Yes, very terrible.* She winced inwardly. Eventually, Mike would warm up to her ideas to simply avoid the more radical changes she was suggesting. Not that Jordan found them outside the realm of possibility, but Mike sure seemed quick to shut her down. She merely wanted to bring the store into the twenty-first century. Expand their online presence, provide more health-conscious and allergen-free foods. Even expand their offerings by enlarging the store to the top floor. All of it would benefit the family as well as the citizens of Willow Springs. Why couldn't Mike see that?

She blew out a breath. *Stop thinking about it.* Still, the thoughts swam around in her head. Jordan wanted to be useful, needed even. Her ex certainly hadn't needed her. Even her ex-roommates—really more childhood friends than anything since she'd known them since her elementary days—had decided they no longer needed her in their lives. What made her think her brother would need her?

Still, he'd been such a huge blessing in letting her come back home. Leaving the home she'd shared with her two friends had seemed like the easiest way to resolve their issues. If Jordan no longer lived there, then her presence would no longer be a problem, and the arguments would cease. The amount she'd made at the boutique meant Jordan couldn't afford to live in Fayetteville on her own. When Michael said she could come home to Willow Springs at any time, relief had flooded her and poured out in tears of gratitude. She'd made an exit strategy and put her heart into making the general store the best it could be.

Only Michael didn't seem to trust her decision-making skills—she was counting Traun as an aberration. If she could just change her brother's mind, Jordan knew he wouldn't be disappointed.

"Jordan?"

Declan's concerned eyes came into view.

"Sorry. What did you say?"

"I asked if you'd be able to come with me on a fishing tour practice." His lips quirked. "I've never done one, and I figure if I can teach a novice, I can guide others."

Her hands flew to her hips. "What makes you think I'm a novice?"

"Come on." He took a step forward, gaze darkening with intensity. "You're telling me you've been fishing?"

Her chin lifted of its own accord. "Guess you'll have to find out, huh?"

There was that look again. If Declan had an ounce of the common sense his grandma had taught him, he'd back up and back down from the challenge showing in Jordan's dark brown gaze. But like times in the past, he didn't listen to that warning and instead, accepted the challenge.

"Fine then." He folded his arms across his chest. "You free Saturday?"

She grinned, as if pleased by the question. "I will be now."

He wanted to chuckle and didn't even know why. "Then I'll pick you up. Be ready."

"What time?"

"I'll pick you up around two."

Her eyes bugged out. "In the morning?"

"No." He let the laughter that had been building loose. "The afternoon. I'm not sure you want to be out in nature at that time. Who knows what's lurking out there?"

She feigned a shudder. "Guess that's why I have you to guide me."

"I'm a guide, not a cop. Don't expect me to keep you safe."

And just like that, some of the joy leeched from her face. Declan examined the words in his mind, trying to find the trigger but couldn't.

"I may have thought fishing happened early in the morning," she said stiffly.

So she was a novice. "Not when it's springtime. Water's too cold for them to be out jumping so early."

Jordan eyed him skeptically. "All right, Mr. Outdoor Adventure. Let's see what you've got."

"Oh, I'll be ready, Ms...." His voice trailed off, unable to finish the comeback. Why did she knock him off his game? He'd been quick with retorts in the past. Hadn't he?

Jordan grinned. "Ms. Expert?"

"No. An expert would've known not to fish in the early uninhabitable hours of the morning."

She scoffed. "Fine. I'm not an expert, but I'm certainly not a novice."

"Sure, Jordan. We'll see about that."

He tipped his ball cap, called out for River and headed out the door without a backward glance. Still, he could feel her gaze piercing him, making the hairs on the back of his neck rise in awareness. The urge to turn around and have one last look pricked at him. Instead, he shut it down and strolled across the lot.

When Declan had woken this morning with the intention of dropping off the new products, he'd had a plan for interacting with Jordan. One that involved not speaking if he could avoid it and not engaging in anything that could be perceived as flirting. He definitely didn't want to give her the impression that he was available. Yet before he'd disappeared from the store, a challenge had been issued, and his plan of avoidance had been aborted.

Something about Jordan Wood screamed *Caution, take cover*, yet he'd still spoken to her. Not very smart on his part. Talking with her was like seeing a Hot sign above a beverage and still checking to see if the item truly packed enough heat to warrant such a warning.

He winced. Bad analogy. Now his mind was cataloging her looks. Jordan was actually the perfect picture of his kryptonite. Short hair that framed a gorgeous face, with a wit and intelligence that made him want to find out who was behind the initial first impression she gave off.

Only the last time he took the time to get to know someone, it had ended in "I do." Declan couldn't afford another bad decision that would make him the main character in a country love song. Though at the moment, he could think of a couple songs about single dads. At least he didn't own a truck to make him the star of a couple more.

As he turned onto Main Street, River piped up from the back. "Where are we going, Dad?"

"Home."

"Do we have to? Can't we go do something fun?"

"Like what?" Should he bring River on the fishing trip Saturday? Declan never took his son on guided excursions, but he'd be a welcome buffer between Declan and Jordan.

"How bout we get some ice cream?" River clapped his hands with excitement.

Declan could afford some soft serve. "Want to go to the Creamery?"

"Yes! I'm going to get the bubble gum kind. No, I think mint. Um, maybe vanilla with sprinkles?"

River began going through the different flavors at Willow Springs's one and only ice cream parlor. He extolled the goodness of chocolate, the toppings one could add to vanilla and why he liked to try various flavors.

When Declan parked in front of the ice cream parlor, his cell phone rang. He swiped left to answer, ignoring the caller ID in favor of time.

"Porter Adventures, this is Declan. How may I help you?" He cleared his throat.

"Don't you ever look at caller ID? I don't need the whole outdoor guide spiel."

His gut clenched. "Mekayla."

"Ugh, do you have to say my name like that? I can hear the disapproval dripping across the waves. What if I'm calling with something good to say?"

He doubted it. "Are you?"

"Depends on your perspective."

"How can I help you?" Declan bit back a sigh, lifting his cap to scratch his head.

"I want to see River for spring break."

He straightened. "What do you mean?"

"You know what I mean."

"Uh, no I don't. Do you want to come out here and see him each day? Take him somewhere? Or…" He was afraid to voice the alternative.

"I want him to come to Oklahoma. My husband wants to meet him."

Declan clenched his teeth. "He barely remembers you," he whispered, glancing at the rearview mirror to see if his son was paying attention to his conversation or still chatting with Nelson the triceratops.

Assured his son was preoccupied, Declan continued. "How do you expect me to get him there?"

"Oh, I can make the drive, no problem. It's only five hours."

"Yeah, if you drive straight through. Don't forget, River's five. Bathroom breaks and snack times are necessary."

She sniffed. "It's still not a big deal."

"Then how about we schedule a video chat? Get him familiar with you again."

"Look, Declan. I don't have time for that. Show him a picture of me and have him ready the Saturday his break starts. According to the school calendar online, that's in a few days. I'll return him the following week."

He wanted to say no. To shout and yell about the unfairness of it all. Only his divorce decree said Mekayla could get spring break and summer vacation, plus every other Thanksgiving and Christmas. This was the first time since the divorce was finalized that she'd actually asked for any of these visitation rights.

Seemed like a lot was changing since she'd remarried on New Year's. Declan could only pray they were good changes. Besides, hadn't he wanted her to see River?

"Fine."

"See? Good news." She hung up.

Time would tell if it really was good news or not. Declan slid his phone into his back pocket, repositioned his cap and swung around to look at River.

"Ready for some ice cream, bud?"

"Yes. Let's go." River unbuckled his seat belt and rocked on his feet while Declan climbed out of the car to let him out.

As River's little hand slipped into his, Declan wanted to squeeze his son and never let go. How was he supposed to tell him his mom—the woman he didn't even remember—wanted to take him away for spring break?

Lord, help.

Chapter Seven

The chicken fried steak had been cooked to perfection. Jordan pushed her plate away with a satisfied smile. There was nothing better than eating at the Sassy Spoon for dinner. What made it extra special, though, was all of the Wood siblings in the booth with her. Mike and Chuck sat across from her and Pippen.

Mike had ordered a burger—his usual choice—and Chuck had eaten a pot pie. Oddly enough, Pippen had pushed her food around with her fork more than she'd eaten. Jordan eyed her little sister, wondering if she was okay. Did her cheeks appear more flushed, or was that just a new blush shade?

"What are you staring at?" Pippen mumbled.

Jordan turned to face her brothers. "Nothing." If something was wrong, Pippen would eventually tell her. She always did.

"Did you finish building the tiny home?" Jordan asked Mike.

"I have a few finishing touches to add before I deem it done. After that, I'll move it."

Mike had been building at the edge of their land so that he didn't disturb anyone with the construction noise.

"So, it'll be in a row on its own?" Pippen asked.

Jordan wanted to mock-shudder. Good thing she didn't have an aerial view of that monstrosity—seeing the solitary configuration would weird her out. If she were Mike, she'd wait until she could move all three new homes. But then again, they'd lose money by not having it available to rent.

"It will, but that'll be fine. The only question is whether to move it to the side with short-term rentals or to the long-term side."

"Short term," Pippen, Chuck and Jordan all said at once.

Mike chuckled. His gaze shifted, and he waved in greeting to someone. Jordan turned, wondering if her brother had spotted Vivian. Instead, she saw Declan and another guy walk in. The guy didn't look like a local. He couldn't be a brother of Declan's, because she would've met him before. Maybe a cousin, but that didn't make sense either. She was pretty sure Declan had mentioned not having other family. But then that meant the guy was a friend. For some reason, imagining Declan having friends, associating with people other than her did something funny to her insides.

Why do you care? It's not like you don't have other friends.

Just then, he caught her gaze, and his mouth quirked up into a semi-smile. She dipped her head in acknowledgment, then turned back into the booth. If only the booth backs had been built higher to block his line of sight. The thought of him staring at her back all evening raised goose bumps on her arms.

"I like them this height," Pippen said.

Jordan could feel her eyes bug out. Had she really mentioned the booth height out loud? Judging from the curious glance in Chuck's eyes and the confusion in Mike's—yep, she really had.

"Do you have a problem with Porter?" Chuck asked.

"She couldn't possibly. They've been working on some secret project," Mike added.

She rolled her eyes. "It's not a secret, I just haven't shared. But no, I don't have a problem with him. We're business associates, that's all."

"What business could you possibly have with him?" Mike leaned forward, brow furrowing.

Jordan wanted to escape the booth as three different pairs of eyes shifted their focus to her face. Heat filled her cheeks as she realized the time had come to tell them about her degree.

She drew in an inhale. "I'm helping him revamp his business." She held her breath as she waited for their reactions.

Mike laughed, his head thrown back in pure pleasure. Chuck's mouth dropped open.

Pippen nudged her. "What do you mean?"

Mike had yet to stop laughing. Jordan's lips pursed as she crossed her arms. "Are you done?"

"You can't be serious?" He wiped at his eyes.

"She looks serious," Chuck said.

"That's because I *am* serious." She expected varying reactions, but not laughter. Part of her heart ached with mortification while the other half was drawing defenses for battle.

"What makes you think you can do that?" Mike asked, incredulity raising his voice.

"How about the bachelor's degree in business with an emphasis on merchandising that has my name on it," she snapped.

Not how she meant to tell them, but oh well. They needed to change their view of her and realize she'd matured.

"When did you get a degree?" Something like hurt flashed in Mike's eyes.

Jordan groaned inwardly. "A year ago."

"Did you walk across the stage?" Chuck asked.

She shook her head.

"So let me get this straight," Mike said, an eyebrow arched. "Not only did you go back to school without telling anyone, but you graduated as well and said nothing? Am I hearing you correctly?"

"Uh-oh," Pippen muttered under her breath.

"I can explain." Jordan held up her hands.

"Please do." Mike settled back in the booth, crossing his arms over his chest.

Ugh. How had things gone from him embarrassing her with his laughter to him being upset she'd kept something like this from him? This was exactly why she'd kept her silence. Nothing was worse than when Mike was upset with her. Yes, he was her older brother, but she also thought of him as a friend.

She shifted in her seat. "I know y'all think I'm a flake who can never keep a job—"

"No I don't," Pippen cried.

"That's not true, Jay." Chuck leaned forward, reaching for her hand.

Instead she moved it back, swiping at the tears that rolled down her cheeks. "Look, when I decided to go back to school, I didn't want to say anything. It was embarrassing knowing I'd lost my scholarship before." Partying and skipping classes would do that to a person.

"Jordan…" Mike sighed, a chagrined expression clouding the happiness she'd begun to see more and more since he'd started dating Vivian.

Jordan ran a hand over the crown of her head. "I only meant to keep quiet for one semester. I wanted to see how it panned out before telling anyone." Plus, she hadn't wanted expectations to weigh her down or cause her to stop her schooling once more.

"Obviously it went well if you graduated, Jay." The hurt look on Chuck's face speared her heart.

Great. She kept her gaze straight, not wanting to see what Pippen's expression said. "Well, yeah. But at the time, I didn't know if doing well that one semester was a fluke." She shrugged her shoulders. "Y'all are so capable at everything you put your minds to. I didn't want to say anything if I couldn't measure up."

"Then Pop died, huh?" Pippen asked.

Jordan eyed her sister, seeing understanding and no judgment in her face. "Exactly. Bringing up my schooling seemed so insignificant then. I just continued taking classes until I had all my credits completed."

"Is this the real reason you have so many

ideas?" Mike asked. "Are you merely trying to put your education to the test?"

She met his stare. "I love the store, Mike, and I love this community. I only wanted to make it better. I'm not trying to step on your toes or insinuate in any way that I know better than you." Having the most current knowledge on merchandising didn't make Jordan better than her brother, but it was her area of expertise. Still, sometimes her enthusiasm came off the wrong way, and she had to be cognizant of the fact.

"Then why not just tell me that?" He threw his hands up.

"Sometimes you don't listen very well," Chuck said. He glanced at Jordan then at Mike. "I imagine she had a fear you'd jump to conclusions or offer unwanted advice if she had."

"Unwanted advice?"

Pippen laughed. "Sometimes, brother, we just want you to listen."

Jordan had never imagined Chuck and Pippen would stick up for her. After all, she'd prevented them all from celebrating her success. Yet at the time, graduating at her age had felt like another failure.

"I'm sorry that I wasn't honest."

Mike ran a hand over his beard and Jordan couldn't help but recall Declan doing that same movement. His blue eyes had flashed as he tried to think of a comeback that failed to make an appearance. Her lips twitched at the memory.

"You're forgiven," Mike said. "I'm sorry I'm not that easy to talk to."

"I love you, brother." Jordan offered him a smile.

"Group hugs," Pippen squealed.

They all spread their arms to reach the next sibling. Moments like this, Jordan missed her parents with a fierceness, but she was thankful to God that he'd left her brothers and a sister to navigate life with.

The Wood siblings were doing some strange group hug, and Declan couldn't tear his eyes away.

"Bro, did you forget I came here to talk, not watch you watch that woman?"

Declan's gaze flew forward, landing on his friend Brendan. Yesterday, Declan had called and invited him to lunch. Brendan had been his college roommate before turning into a friend. Though they talked from time to time, he'd never visited Willow Springs before.

"I kind of got the impression over the phone that you were desperate?" Brendan tapped his fingers on the tabletop.

Declan let out a strained laugh. "Not desperate per se. I need advice, and since you're a lawyer…" Why was this so hard?

"What's going on?"

"Mekayla wants River for the week of spring break." Declan ran a hand through his hair. "Only he's never met her. She's never tried to enact her visitation rights since she left. So…" Again his voice broke off.

Brendan grimaced. "Sadly, it doesn't matter if she's never used her visitation rights before. If they're written in your divorce decree, then you have to follow them."

Declan sat back in his chair. "How am I supposed to explain that to River?"

"Has he ever expressed an interest in knowing her?"

"Of course, man. He's a kid who knows other people have moms."

"Then maybe he'll be excited." Brendan shrugged. "Talk her up, remember the good points and share those with him."

Declan ran a hand down his face. *The good points?* What were those again? Instead of voicing his thoughts out loud, he simply nodded. If he couldn't stop Mekayla from taking River, then Declan would do everything in his power to ensure his son wasn't apprehensive about the visit.

"Thanks," he said.

"No problem. Now tell me about the woman." Brendan hooked a thumb over his shoulder.

"Bro," he muttered, his neck feeling uncomfortably warm.

"What?" Brendan asked, eyebrows raised innocently. "You've been staring at her since she made eyes at you."

Declan shook his head. "No, it's not like that. Jordan is helping me with some business matters. We're like coworkers."

Brendan turned around in his seat. "I need coworkers like that."

"Stop." Declan reached over, nudging his friend. "Behave."

"I will." Brendan faced forward. "She's coming over. Mission accomplished."

Lord, why? Declan would give anything to shake Brendan and ask him why he would torture Declan like that. But there was no time. Jordan stood a couple of feet from their table.

"Hey, Declan."

"Jordan." He nodded. "This is my friend Brendan. Brendan, this is Jordan."

"Nice to meet you." Brendan smiled flirtatiously.

Declan's gut clenched as Jordan returned the smile. Did interest gleam in her eyes? *Why do you care?*

"Sibling lunch, huh?" He groaned to himself. Could his question be any more basic?

"Yeah, it's rare for us all to be in the same place lately. Pip came for her spring break, so…" She shrugged.

"Hope you're enjoying your lunch."

"Maybe I can take you to dinner?" Brendan said at the same time.

Declan grunted, trying to suppress his words and his body from jumping up all at the same time. Only the noise must have been loud enough to catch his friend and Jordan's attention because their heads swiveled toward him.

"Are we still on for the great fishing challenge, Mr. Porter?" She placed a hand on her hip.

"Bring it, little novice." He narrowed his gaze in good fun.

Judging by the half-smile, Jordan caught his mood. She squinted her eyes as well and made a motion with her hands as if to punch him. "I'll bring it and you'll eat my dirt."

He choked down laughter.

"Fishing challenge?" Brendan asked.

Declan looked at his friend. "Ms. Wood thinks she's better at fishing than me."

"And this Neanderthal," Jordan quipped, "thinks women can't fish."

"Not true." He paused. "I don't think *you* can fish."

Her nose flared. "Winner takes all?"

"All what?" He gave himself a mental kick in the rear. Why couldn't he have said something better?

Jordan laughed, shaking her head. "See you soon, Declan. Nice to meet you, Brendan."

His friend stared, bemused. As soon as Jordan was out of earshot, Brendan looked Declan straight in the eyes. "You like her, and she likes you."

Declan spewed his drink all over the table. "No, I don't." He grabbed a napkin, mopping up his mess.

"She didn't even answer me when I asked her out," Brendan said with a smirk.

"She probably didn't hear you."

"She heard and rejected me by asking you about the fishing challenge. And I'm still not sure what's happening with that." Brendan took a casual bite of his food.

Was this the point where Declan was supposed to admit he had no idea what to say either? He already felt foolish that he lost his sparring wits whenever Jordan was around, and now Brendan had witnessed that tragedy.

"She's helping me create and test new tours for my business. She's like a guinea pig."

Brendan snorted. "Yeah right. Has River met her?"

"Of course. Willow Springs is small."

"Maybe I should be more specific."

Declan draped an arm on the back of his chair, feigning disinterest. "I don't know what you mean."

"Has River had a meal with Jordan?"

"N-no."

"Aha!" Brendan pointed a finger at him. "That's a real yes, but my question wasn't specific enough." He glanced over his shoulder then back at Declan. "I'm guessing some of her family was in attendance."

Declan's jaw flexed.

Brendan nodded slowly, a Cheshire cat grin forming. "So, you've met the family."

"Bro, stop. Trust me. It's not like that. If you lived in Willow Springs, you'd get it. We're a tight-knit community. Everyone helps everyone. It was nothing more than that."

"Sure, Declan. Keep telling yourself that."

He would. Because there was no way he would ever date Jordan. Declan didn't trust himself to pick the right woman—just look at the evidence against him. Not to mention what it could do to River. If he was attached to Jordan already as just a member of the community, how would he feel if they dated then broke up? Besides, she was too… And well, Declan was too…

Simply put, they would be a disaster. And Declan wasn't completely healed from the disaster that was Mekayla. How could he ever trust another woman not to abandon him again?

"I'm not dating, man. My focus remains on my son and my business. That's it."

"That's not realistic. What happens if you meet that one woman who knocks you off kilter, and you discover life is better with her around?"

That sounded terrible. Declan wanted a stable life with no drama. He thought a divorce certificate would be the beginning of a more secure life. He never imagined Mekayla popping back up to ask for money and then coming back once more to demand River's presence. Just when he thought he could breathe again, she had new demands. What would adding a girlfriend do to that?

"I'm good how I am, Brendan."

"Yet you were ready to fight me when I asked out Jordan." Brendan spread his hands out, nonverbally asking, *Do you disagree?*

Declan wanted to with every fiber in his being. "I was just a little concerned."

Brendan laughed. "Yeah, a little concerned she'd say yes and you'd be watching from the sidelines." Brendan slapped the table. "Don't worry, man. I would've never gone through with it if she'd said yes."

"She didn't say yes."

"Because she shot me down and looked at the real object of her affection."

Declan shook his head, but he had no more words. Brendan lived in an alternate world and Declan wasn't going to play that game.

"Thanks for the lunch," Brendan said. "I think I'll head back home."

"You sure? I figured we'd hang out some more."

"Nah," Brendan said. "You have a son and a lady to decide if you want to make something happen with." He spread out his hands. "And I have basketball to watch."

"Then I appreciate you coming out. Next time, I'll just make a phone call so I don't pry you away from the game."

Brendan laughed. "Give me a free tour package, and I'll come back out sooner than you think."

"I've got you."

Brendan clapped him on the back and Declan watched as his friend left. His gaze caught the Woods heading for the door.

There was no way Brendan was right. Jordan Wood couldn't possibly see anything of interest in him, right? As if she read his thoughts, she turned, capturing his gaze. With a wink and a wave, she sauntered out of the diner.

Declan would need to shore up his defenses before he went fishing with her. Who knew what the idea of them together—*thanks a lot Brendan*—would do to his psyche when they were fishing? He'd just have to remember it was a trial run on how he'd treat real tourists.

You've got this. He gave himself a mental fist pump then left to get his son.

Chapter Eight

Life had taken a strange turn. The whole time she'd been living in Willow Springs these past three months—just in time to celebrate Christmas, and now spring was showing up—Jordan had never noticed or interacted with Declan. So why, now, did she keep seeing him at the Sassy Spoon, the general store, his house, midweek Bible study, etc.?

Here she stood at the post office to mail something, and in walked Declan. If she looked straight ahead, would he figure out it was her or assume she was someone else?

A tap on her shoulder and a whispered, "Hey" answered that question.

She gulped, then glanced over her shoulder. "Hey, Mr. Adventure."

"Oh, you dropped the 'outdoor,' huh?" His blue eyes glinted with amusement.

"It was implied."

"Right," he drew out.

For the first time, she noticed a Southern inflection in his words. "Where's your sidekick?"

"Brendan went back home. He's not a Willow Springs resident."

She smirked.

"Oh, you meant River, didn't you?"

"Yep." She took a step forward as someone left the line.

"He's at school. Though tomorrow is his first day of break." Something that looked strangely like sorrow darkened his blue eyes.

Searching to lighten the mood, Jordan said, "Tomorrow is Saturday. Does that count as the first day of vacation?"

"Weren't you a kid once, or have you always had this adult air about you?"

Having her mother pass when Jordan was young had made a big impact on her growing up early. She couldn't quite figure out what emotion went through her right now or why his question triggered a flashback. "My childhood didn't seem as long as others'."

An understanding gaze met hers. "I get that," he whispered softly.

Of course he did, having been raised by his grandma. Jordan tilted her head. "What happened to your parents?" she asked quietly.

"Grandma said my mother dropped me off in a basket with a note. She expected my dad to be home, but he had died a few months prior in a work accident. I only had my grandma."

Her stomach twisted at the thought. Though both of her parents were no longer here, at least she'd had them in her life versus not at all. "I can't imagine what that must have been like."

His chin touched his chest. "There were difficult days. I spent plenty of time wondering if it was something I did to make my mom leave." He lifted his head, and the pain in his eyes pierced her. "Somehow I seemed to have repeated history. I never wanted River to experience life without a mom."

The ache from Jordan's stomach seemed to have traveled throughout her body, landing in her throat. "Oh, Declan, I'm so sorry. When I broke up with my ex, my mom was the first person I wanted to call. It hurts, her absence." She bit her lip. She hadn't meant to share that tidbit.

Why not? He's sharing so much with you, after all.

She cleared her throat. "I get why you wouldn't want that for him."

"I knew you'd understand," he said quietly.

Instinct had her wanting to offer to be there for River, but self-preservation kept her silent. "When did your grandma pass?"

"After River was born."

So much loss. How could one man handle that? Suddenly, the sadness that always seemed to hover over Declan made so much more sense. Before she could make another comment, he cleared his throat and pointed ahead. "You're next."

Right. She'd almost forgotten they were in the post office while Declan had been spilling secrets. She gulped and moved to the next available window. "Hi, can I mail this priority?" Jordan pushed the small box onto the counter.

Yesterday she'd unpacked the last box she'd brought with her in the move. In it were a few things that belonged to her ex-roommates. In the rush to leave a bad situation, she must have shoved their belongings into her box by mistake. Sending the items back would hopefully close that painful chapter in her life. The one where her roommates chose Traun over her.

Who decided it was okay to share a man, and if the third woman didn't agree, kick her out? Sure, Jordan probably could've made a big stink since her name had been on the lease right along with theirs. But at the time, it seemed more prudent to remove herself from their lives and simply pick up the pieces. Her landlord had been understanding and gave no penalty for her moving out since the other two women were staying and moving in Traun in her stead.

Still, the thought of mailing off this box made everything feel so final. Made her want to grab a blanket, some comfort food and take up space on her couch to binge-watch a mindless movie or TV series.

Jordan paid the postage, then hustled out the door. She didn't look at Declan or wave goodbye. Sharing personal details with him had added a level of vulnerability she hadn't been expecting. The moment she got to her car, her phone chimed. A notification reminder flashed: *Fishing with Declan.* Jordan groaned. That was tomorrow. Making a one-eighty, Jordan took a couple of steps toward the post office once more. Just then, Declan exited the building.

She waved a hand in the air. "Declan!" she yelled.

He froze, gaze scanning the parking lot. She waved again from where she'd parked. His eyes lit in recognition then he crossed the lot.

"What's up?"

"Are we still on for fishing tomorrow? You did say River will be on spring break. I don't want to encroach on your time with him."

Declan's face paled. "Uh, yeah. Um, he's going to be out of town."

She raised her eyebrows. "Is everything okay?"

"Yep. Good. Just fine." His feet shifted on the asphalt. "I, uh, I'll still pick you up tomorrow."

"Okay." Something was wrong, but they didn't have quite that intimate of a relationship where Jordan could pry.

He just told you about his parents.

Still, she needed to respect his boundaries. Plus, she had to get back to the store and get ready to open it for the afternoon shift. "See you tomorrow, Declan."

"Bye."

Jordan made herself get in the car, trying to ignore the misery she'd glimpsed on Declan's face. When he moved a few cars down to get into his Jeep, she placed her head on the steering wheel.

"Lord, I don't know what's going on with Declan," she whispered. "But I ask for You to comfort him. Please let the Holy Spirit intercede on his behalf. Please bless him. Bless River. Please help them in whatever way they need. Amen."

Jordan couldn't help but feel some kind of way toward Declan and River. Was it knowing Declan was in a financial bind that made her think about him more than she should? Or maybe the fact that he was a single father trying to do the best he could softened her toward them? Certainly, all he'd shared in the post office had turned her heart to putty. Almost made her tear ducts work as well. Not to mention the cuteness scale that was all River Porter.

His affection for dinosaurs and humor toward life made Jordan think that kids weren't so bad after all. She always figured she'd be an awful mother, what with no mom to guide her or even Pop around to offer parental advice. Talking with River and making him smile was as easy as breathing.

And admitting all of those emotions made her want to hide away and cancel her fishing excursion. Yet, she couldn't leave Declan in the lurch when she'd promised to help his business flourish. She was the one who told him to add more tour packages to his company. She owed it to him to ensure that the fishing trip would be another adventure worthy of his brand. Besides, she had until tomorrow to cement it in her mind that this was all strictly business between them. Praying for him didn't mean she *liked him* liked him, but simply cared as a fellow believer.

Right, Lord?

How did Saturday arrive so quickly? Declan had done all he could to prepare River and get him used to what his mother looked like. Declan had pulled out an old photo album with pictures from when he and Mekayla had first started dating. It had been stored in a box specifically for River for when he decided to take a deeper interest in the woman who gave him life. Sometime far in the future, Declan had presumed. He'd prayed that by then, River's sense of abandonment would wane, but maybe it was actually Declan's that needed to dissipate.

Mekayla had hurt him on a level of pain he never thought possible. Now his heart felt like it was being ripped in half once more. Preparing his child to be without him for a week seemed so contrary to God's design. One of those times that "broken world" was so apt and so annoying for not being just a cliché and pithy statement but a reality for him.

He'd tried asking Mekayla to reconsider. To introduce herself slowly to River instead of carting him off for a week, but she refused to think about anyone but herself. Which was why she was knocking at the front entrance right then. He said a quick prayer for patience and grace, then opened the door.

"Mekayla." She wore a flowing dress and had her makeup artfully applied. But not an ounce of attraction sprang up upon seeing her. Declan would count that as a small victory.

She smirked, flipping her long brown hair over her shoulder. "Where's River?"

"He's inside. Would you like to come in?" Did he get bonus points for being nice?

"If I must."

She trounced into his home, the one place that wasn't drenched in memories of her or their old way of life. Hopefully, her presence wouldn't disturb his peace once she left…again.

River sat on the couch and froze when Mekayla walked up to him. "River, darling. Come with me."

Instead, he ran toward Declan, wrapping his arms around his leg. Declan angled himself in order to pat his boy on the back, praying he would feel comfort. "River, remember what we talked about? This is your mom."

He nodded, clutching Nelson to his chest.

"Are you ready to go?" Mekayla asked.

"Can Dad come?" River asked quietly.

"No. Besides—" She grinned, smoothing her hands over her stomach and revealing a small baby bump. "I've got so much to tell you."

Declan's gaze shot to hers. "Why didn't you say something? I could have prepared him."

She folded her arms across her chest. "I *am* his mother, Dec. I can tell him about my life without your help."

Yeah, but what exactly would she say? Didn't she understand she was basically a stranger to River?

"Come on, River, let's go." She clapped her hands. "Hawk is ready to head home."

Declan kneeled down and hugged his son close. "I love you, bud. I'll call you tonight, okay?"

"I don't wanna go," River murmured into Declan's neck, his little arms clinging to him.

"This will be a good chance to hang out with your mom, 'kay? You'll be just fine. Remember, you have Nelson to keep you company, and God is always watching over you." *Lord, please watch over my boy. I know You love him more than me, so I trust You and what that means for this moment.*

"What about you? I want you," said River.

"Stop babying him, Dec." Mekayla picked River up. "Let's go. You'll see your dad next week."

"Dad!" River stretched out his arms.

The cry sliced Declan in two. He watched them walk out of the house, feeling like his heart went with them as well.

He rushed forward, stopping in the doorway. "I'll call you, bud. I love you. Be brave." He swallowed, hating the heaving motion going on in his stomach.

Mekayla strapped River into a booster, and then her husband drove off with Declan's kid. Not *theirs*, but *his* son. The one he taught to walk, learn the alphabet, write and read. Declan had been there for every first, while his ex was who knew where.

Slowly, he closed the door, leaning his head against the frame. The silence threatened to drown him. How was he supposed to make it seven days without his boy?

Declan's watch beeped and he took note of the time. It was a little early to pick up Jordan—okay, two hours early—but he couldn't stay in this house one minute longer. He'd do nothing but sit in River's room and miss his endless chatter.

I'll never complain about him talking me to death again. Declan would give anything to hear his son go on and on about dinosaurs. He'd even listen to his argument about how he could save them despite them being extinct. Declan needed to burn off some energy. Too bad he didn't own a punching bag.

He headed for his shed in the backyard. Grabbing the gear they'd need, Declan laid it all out in the Jeep. He double-checked everything with a mental list before calling it good. Saying a quick prayer, Declan asked the Lord to pave a way for him. Would Jordan be annoyed by his early arrival? Only time would tell.

After parking in front of the general store, Declan unclipped his cell from its holder. He probably should have messaged Jordan before leaving his house. *Oh well.*

Declan: Any chance you can go fishing now?

Jordan: Where's the fire?

He huffed. *In his heart.* Only that answer was all too real.

Declan: Down by the river.

Jordan: Is that a song title? Sounds like one.

Why did this woman make him want to pull out his hair?

Declan: Can you leave or not?

Jordan: Excuse me, Mr. Adventure. Won't you be happy to know I'm already ready.

His eyebrows raised. Why? Was she looking forward to fishing? Could she really know something about it already?

Declan: Great. I'm parked outside.

Jordan: Wow. Eager much?

He laughed out loud, and the band that had squeezed his chest since Mekayla waltzed back into his life loosened. Not to mention he no longer felt like tugging his hair from his scalp.

Declan: What can I say? Your sunny disposition hooked me.

Declan: See what I did there?

Jordan: I'm trying not to, but apparently, this isn't a vanishing text.

Another bark of laughter escaped his lips. He put the phone back into the cupholder and relaxed, waiting for Jordan to come out. Before he could get comfortable, the front door opened, and she strolled across the lot. She wore blue jean overalls and a black tee underneath. What was more surprising than the overalls was the fishing cap perched on her head.

She opened the Jeep's passenger door and tossed her pack on the floor before sliding onto the seat. "Good morning, sunshine."

He grunted on purpose.

"Hmm. Just as I thought. You apparently need some outdoor time."

"Truer words have never been spoken." He shoved the gear in Drive and headed out.

At first, he welcomed the silence. Soon, however, Declan began fidgeting in his seat. Finally, he let out an exhale and spoke. "Go ahead and ask."

"Ask what?"

"What's gotten into me?"

"Obviously, something's stuck in your craw. You're pricklier than a pine."

Declan looked at her, rolled his eyes, then faced the road once more. Jordan just laughed, the sound reminiscent of a wind chime.

"No really. What's wrong?"

"My ex has *my* son." His jaw clenched, and he focused on inhaling and exhaling slowly.

"Wow. How long has it been since you've seen her?"

His hands clenched the wheel. "Four years." Give or take a couple of months.

"Oh wow." Silence filled the interior once more.

Declan peeked at Jordan and saw deep lines etched into her forehead.

"Does that mean River hasn't seen her since he was a baby?" she asked quietly.

"Yep." Declan's lips popped at the word.

"How did he handle the reunion?"

"Not well. Wanted me there with him. I at least had the foresight to ensure he took a stuffed animal with him. He chose Nelson.

Clutched him like he'd never let go." Declan rubbed the back of his neck.

Jordan squeezed his forearm briefly. The shock of her touch left him mute, but she started talking as if nothing had transpired.

"I'm so sorry, Declan. I can't imagine how hard that must've been."

He cleared his throat. "Yeah, well, I never imagined Mekayla would've left me to go find herself and end up finding someone else instead." Wasn't that the kicker? Deep down, he thought she'd come back to him. But after two years, all he got was divorce paperwork.

"It's not your fault."

He snorted. "It's what I tell River but absolutely don't believe it for myself." He ran a hand over his face. Why was he spilling his guts? "Sorry, I don't mean to overshare." Yet something had released inside of him when he'd told her part of his story at the post office. Jordan Wood was surprisingly easy to talk to. Not that he'd ever admit that to her.

"There's nothing to apologize for. Sometimes we just need to get our worries out of our mind. They take up less space that way."

"Such wise words." He tossed a smirk her way, trying to lighten a mood his emotions had brought down. "I'm curious as to what kind of worries you've experienced to give you that knowledge."

A bitter chuckle fell from her lips. "Sometimes the hits just keep coming. I'm not sure you want to hear my drama."

She'd let a little slip yesterday. He might have wondered how bad the breakup was before worry of Mekayla and spring break took over. "Try me," he said.

"How about a two-timing—wait, make that *three*-timing—boyfriend. One who decided to cheat on me with my *two* best friends, aka my roommates. And one of them ended up pregnant." She blew out a breath. "Too bad that's not even the kicker."

"It's not?" Could this sound any more like reality TV?

"Nope. My two ex-friends decided to continue dating him. When I tried to get them to see the error of their ways, they let me know where the exit was."

Declan let out a low whistle. "So, that's why you came back to Willow Springs?" He spared a quick glance her way.

"Yes." Sorrow etched itself deep into her eyes.

If he squeezed her arm like she had his, would she welcome the touch or become uncomfortable? Declan sharpened his focus on the road.

"I wanted no part of that drama, and I *refuse*

to believe it's my fault." Her voice rose as she continued to vent. "Some people are takers, and no amount of goodness on your part will change them into anything else. The *only* fault I claim is not recognizing what type of man he was in the first place."

Declan could completely relate to that. "I should've known Mekayla would flake out on me and River. She always had trouble making decisions. When she did make a choice, it was always one that benefited her or had a materialistic outcome in her favor." He squeezed the steering wheel.

Why had he been so foolish over her? Look what it had cost him and River.

"What did y'all have in common?" Jordan asked softly.

"I can honestly say nothing. Back then, I didn't think it was a big deal." He rubbed his chin. "Now I realize how there are deeper issues a man and woman need to be aligned on besides what your hobbies are."

"I agree. I let Traun's charm blind me to his faults." Jordan shifted in her seat. "Do you think you'll ever marry again?"

He started shaking his head once she said *marry.* "No way. I plan on staying single and devoting my time to raising River."

"I hear ya. I'm focusing on getting my life

right. Being single will allow me to do so without worrying about what someone else thinks."

"Exactly. I tell my friend that all the time." He glanced at her. "But your life is a little less complicated. If you decided to date again, you could. Whereas I'm a single father, and River will always factor into my future decisions."

"Yes, but that doesn't mean your future girlfriend or wife would necessarily make matters complicated. Surely there are plenty of women who would willingly be a good stepmom. Brighten up y'all's day."

He wanted to laugh at the thought. *Wow, am I really that bitter?* He swallowed. "Well, I'm sure there are genuine guys out there. Ones who only want one woman." But why did the thought of Jordan dating someone have his gut clenching?

"I don't know. I don't have a good track record in the relationship department."

"You and me both."

Jordan chuckled and they settled into silence. This time, the urge to break it didn't overwhelm Declan. He actually felt a little better. Maybe Jordan had a point about getting the worry out of his head. Now he could focus on fishing and try to enjoy the rest of his day.

Only he still missed River with every fiber of his being. *Look after him, please, Lord. Please.*

Chapter Nine

❦

Okay, so Jordan had fished before. In her book, that meant she wasn't a novice. However, she *definitely* was no expert. Last night, she'd had a conversation with Mike, asking him for help on recalling all the tips Pop had given them on fishing trips. Mike had remembered a little more than she, so now Jordan came prepared to impress Declan.

Not that she *needed* to impress him. She only wanted to see that look of surprise on his face when he realized how much he'd underestimated her.

Sure, keep telling yourself that.

She absolutely did not care if Declan thought her capable. *Did. Not!* So she stood in the river, waders on and pole in hand. The trickling sound of the water attempted to soothe her mind, but the angst rolling off Declan had Jordan searching for something to say. Plus it gave her time to ignore the surprising call she'd received from her old roommate. Anything to forget about that. Focusing on Declan and River's current predicament was a better use of her time. How could she help Declan through his separation from River?

Just the thought of his ex showing up out of the blue, demanding River go along with her burned Jordan up. Yes, there were probably lawful visitation rights in the mix, but you didn't make yourself scarce for four years while your child grew up not knowing you, and then expect to be welcomed with open arms. Something seemed off in the scenario, but Jordan would keep that thought to herself.

Jordan's pole jerked and she gasped. "Declan, I got a bite." Her voice came out breathy with excitement and just a little higher than normal.

"Reel it in, then." He smirked, his eyes practically screaming, *I double-dog dare you.*

Jordan lifted her chin. "I will." She shifted her gaze, recalling Pop's calms words: *Keep a steady hold. Don't panic or the fish will win.*

"I'm steady, Pop," she murmured. Though her breath came in spurts, her hands worked in an orderly fashion to reel in her prize.

Her eyes widened as the fish broke the surface, wriggling around. Jordan squealed, barely containing her excitement. She'd actually caught a fish. It'd been years since she'd been fishing, and this was her first time standing in the river to accomplish the feat.

Earlier, Declan had been calm and confident when he'd explained the gear and gave her tips. However, the glint in his eyes clearly meant he believed her a novice and not an experienced fisher. Still, she'd listened to his spiel, knowing he was trying to ensure he could provide a good experience for tourists. Catching a fish made those earlier boring moments worth it.

As she took the fish off the hook, Jordan held it up in triumph. "Take a pic, please!"

Declan set his pole in a holder then pulled out his cell phone. "Smile."

"Fishing!" she exclaimed.

He chuckled then pocketed the phone. "I'll text it to you later."

"Sounds good." She scanned the area. "Where's the cooler?"

"Over there." He pointed behind him.

Jordan deposited the fish on ice and went back to her pole to start all over.

They stayed in the river a couple more hours until Declan called it quits. The final catch total was Jordan four and Declan three. That was enough to keep a smile on her face.

After shedding her waders, she got into his

vehicle and looked at him. "What are you going to do with them?"

"Eat 'em. I'm a huge fan of fried fish."

So was she. "Who isn't?" Just thinking of the food had her mouth salivating as she imagined the taste.

"River." Declan's smile dimmed. "He always makes the most obnoxious gagging noises when I fry fish."

"Kids. They have no taste."

Declan laughed outright. "Tell me about it. If I have to make or eat another PB&J, I might cry. If you see tears, pretend my eyes are watering and look the other way."

Delight flitted through Jordan at his humor. When Declan got to talking, his personality really shone through. It was a shame it only piqued her interest more in him. Something about his quiet demeanor made her want to know his thoughts. Were they as quiet as his outward appearance, or did he have thousands of questions going through his mind?

"What are you thinking about?" The question popped out freely, but Jordan wanted to snatch it back. She didn't want to entertain this awareness that kept seeing Declan Porter in a new light.

She wanted to stick to her plan to help him grow his business and prove to Mike—and herself—that she had what it took in the business world. She wanted to shed the stench of failure, of moving from one job to the next, and show that she could put to use the degree she'd worked so hard for. She wanted Mike to loosen his hold on running the general store and trust that Jordan was perfectly capable of managing the place. She certainly didn't need to moon over a guy and his cute kid, imagining an alternate life where they could build new dreams together.

Declan flicked a glance her way before facing the road. "I'm wondering if River is having a good time. Wondering if Mekayla has an ulterior motive I simply can't figure out. Wondering if she's going to ask for joint custody. Or worse, that she'll bail again, and I'll have to explain to River why her issues are not his fault." He blew out a breath.

Yep. A thousand questions running through his head. Somehow that only endeared him to her more. *No, no, no! Single and drama free, remember?*

Baby mama drama was definitely something Jordan wanted to avoid. Hadn't she just leapt from that fire, leaving her two roommates behind? They'd have to fight for her ex's attention and raise a baby in that nontraditional environment. No, thank you. Jordan did *not* want that for herself.

If she ever married—and that was a huge if considering the heartache she'd gone through with Traun—Jordan prayed the guy would have Pop's integrity. She would only marry one man and have whatever number of kids God blessed them with. Only these days, that seemed like a far-fetched dream. When had dating become so difficult and started feeling so hopeless?

Am I supposed to remain single, God? Is that thought just a sign that I'm tired of the performance of putting my best foot forward only to have it yanked from under me when the guy turns out to be not good enough to date?

Or did God really want her to remain single and serve Him with her purpose?

Which was what again? Using her degree at the store—or something else she hadn't yet figured out?

She studied Declan's profile. He *seemed* like a good man, but so had Traun when she'd first met him.

"Hey, Jordan?"

"Yes?"

"Want to come over and have some fish? I'm sure I have stuff to make coleslaw." Did she detect a hidden vulnerability in his question?

"Swing by the store and I'll grab something to make hush puppies." Because that was the perfect accompaniment to a fish fry.

"Oh, I already have premade batter."

"What do you mean 'premade'?" She eyed him. "Like a mix you bought at the store?" The general store had some sitting on the shelves.

"Nah, this was made from a recipe my grandma had. She taught me how to mix it ahead and store it in an airtight container. That way I'd be able to make some whenever I want."

Curiouser and curiouser. Declan had many hidden layers to himself. If only Jordan could stop noticing them and wanting to peel them back.

She refocused on the plan ahead. "Sounds like a great idea. Anyone else we should invite?" Pippen had returned to school, so Jordan couldn't call her, but maybe Chuck would be interested.

"You don't have to, unless Big Mike wants to come," Declan suggested.

"He and Vivian are out on a day date."

"A day date?"

She nodded. Those two would be sickening if they weren't so sweet.

Okay, so she was purely jealous. "They're trying to do things that foster them getting to know each other much better, but also because they both work during the week, they often can't hang out for long periods of time." Jordan wiped her hands on her overalls. "They'll start out having breakfast together, then spend the day doing whatever. From my understanding, it was Vivian's turn to plan their day this time."

"That's interesting. Do they spend the evening together as well?"

"Yep. Dinner ends the date. Mike says they're taking things slow." Vivian wanted to reach a year of sobriety before they dated seriously.

But Jordan couldn't differentiate between serious dating and spending the day together. Isn't that what serious couples did? Maybe she was missing something.

"Slow is good. If I had taken that advice, I probably wouldn't be in the situation I'm in with my ex."

"But would you have River?"

He sighed. "Ain't that the kicker? Prime example of God using all for good. River is all that's good in my world."

"Just River?" she asked softly. She could understand focusing on the brightest spot. But what happened if you didn't see light in your surroundings?

Wow, Lord. How often have I bemoaned my life and never took the chance to count You as a blessing? Shame coursed through her.

"Not only him. I have a job I love. I'm part of a community I love." Declan shrugged.

"Do you love it? Because I never see you chat

with anyone at church. And if I hadn't met Brendan, I would have assumed you had no friends." She winced inwardly at the last part. Sometimes her mouth truly ran away with her. "Sorry. That was rude. Please forgive me."

"No, no. You have a good point." Declan sighed, running his hand through his hair. Halfway home, he'd ditched the ball cap that was almost always perched on his head.

"I'm usually on the fringes of the community," he continued. "Been that way most of my life. Not because I don't love Willow Springs, I'm just not sure how to engage with anyone. I've spent so much time on the outside looking in, I don't know how to jump into the fray."

"Recklessly," she quipped.

Declan laughed.

"Seriously though. Talk to people. Greet them. Or find an extrovert and let them drag you around town and into the fray, so to speak."

"Do you know a willing extrovert?"

"Hello!" She pointed to herself, then inwardly smacked the back of her head.

Increasing her time with Declan wouldn't help her thoughts stay in the business arena if she began doing nonbusiness activities with him. She needed to keep her head focused on consulting and nothing more. No more questions about his life or River or anything that would soften her heart.

Did you forget the fish fry? Because you're doing such a wonderful job of maintaining boundaries.

Something happened. One minute Jordan was all smiles and chatting a mile a minute. The next, her smiled dropped as swiftly as the temperature in the dead of winter. Declan glanced her way, puzzled by the lines etched in her forehead.

"You all right?"

"Um, yeah." She cleared her throat, shaking her head. "What were we talking about again?"

"Me joining the world of the living."

She chuckled and his heart lightened. Maybe she'd just had a bad thought or something. He could relate to that. All day his mind kept flitting to River, but each time, Jordan would reel him back in with her questions.

"Well, there are plenty of extroverts to help you with that. You'll be able to spot them by their enthusiasm for interacting with humans."

Declan opened his mouth, then shut it. He got the feeling Jordan Wood didn't want to hang out with him outside of business hours. At first, it felt like shades of high school all over again. The popular girl ignoring anyone who wasn't in the same crowd as she. But a deeper assessment proved he was okay with the lines being drawn.

He had a son to raise, a business to improve and money to find growing on trees—or *somewhere*. Hanging out with Jordan would only complicate his life. How could he trust her to stick around—even if only as a friend—when so many of the women in his life had left already? All he had was River, and making sure his son never felt neglected would take all of Declan's energy. His life already had so many complications, and Jordan might as well have *complicated* written in neon lights across her forehead. Declan just wanted to live a simple life, free of headaches.

Is that even possible?

Maybe not. He'd already added *divorcé, single parent* and *business owner* to his life list. Each of those brought a complexity he'd never prepared for or even thought of as a teen. Declan had dreamed of a stress-free life that allowed him to do something he loved but would also pay for his expenses. Including the expenses needed to raise a family. His teen imagination could never have dreamt up his current life.

How wrong he'd been about it all.

Declan ran a hand across his chin, then pulled into the driveway. "I'll grab the gear. You can head into the house if you want."

"How about I get the cooler?" Jordan gazed into his eyes. "I can start cleaning the fish so you can get all the gear situated."

His mouth dropped. "You know how to clean fish?"

"Of course. One of the first things Pop taught me."

Considering she'd caught more fish than he had, Declan might as well admit defeat. Jordan Wood was not a novice or apparently a woman who squealed at the idea of cleaning dead fish. Still, he'd pay money to see her gut and clean one.

"That would be helpful. I usually clean them in my shed. There's a sink and everything."

"I'm on it."

Declan unlocked the shed and held it open for Jordan. She headed straight for the counter near the sink. If he hustled back and forth between the car and the shed, he should be able to see her gut at least two or three fish.

He hightailed it to his vehicle, grabbing item after item. He set them in the shed, then went back out for another run. The last run, he came in just in time to see Jordan peel off the catfish's skin. Then she sliced him up, gutting him.

Lord, who knew a woman cleaning fish could be an attractive sight?

His face heated at the thought.

She looked up and smiled. "Hey. I'm almost done cleaning them. You want to take these inside and fry them?"

He actually needed to clean his gear, but maybe he could do that once Jordan left. As long as he didn't forget, it should be fine to hold off an hour or two.

"Place them in the cooler, and I'll bring them to the house."

She scrubbed her hands, then followed him out of the shed and through the French doors at the back of the house. Declan slipped off his boots and placed them to the side of the entryway. He'd move them to the shoe rack in the foyer later.

"Should I take mine off too?" Jordan asked.

"Please."

Declan set the cooler down on the counter, then grabbed the cornmeal from the pantry and some spices from the cabinet holding all the seasonings.

"Should I make the hush puppies?"

"No, that's okay. I'll do it."

Jordan placed her hands on her hips. "Then what else can I do, Declan? The fish are done."

Declan peered around his kitchen. He didn't want her touching Grandma's hush puppy mix. That seemed like something a wife would do. *Then what does that leave her?*

"Uh, wanna get the fish ready to fry?"

"Sure." She nodded to the spices in his arm. "What kind do you have?"

"Salt, pepper—the usual."

Jordan smirked. "Let's have a cooking competition."

"How so?"

"I'll dress some and you do the others. Then we'll see whose taste better."

Declan tilted his head. "What's the prize?"

Jordan's grin widened. Lines framing her mouth and a gleaming smile only added to her joyful expression. "Winner has to divulge a secret no one knows."

His stomach tensed. What more could he share with Jordan? Wasn't it bad enough she knew about his childhood abandonment, failed marriage and fledgling business? It was like she was out for blood. Still, she had shared with him as well. It couldn't have been easy to admit her ex cheated on her...with both of her roommates.

Since he knew he made the best fish in Willow Springs—even had a blue ribbon from the time River encouraged him to participate in the summer fish fry—Declan agreed to her terms. "Fine."

Jordan proffered her hand, and he shook it.

He pointed to the cooler. "Grab the first four, and I'll work on the other three."

She smirked. "You mean my winning four?"

"Yeah, yeah," he mumbled. He grabbed his and went to work in a separate part of the kitchen to give himself a little more room.

"I'll fry my own too," Jordan called over her shoulder.

"Fine. I'll make the hush puppies when you do that."

"Sounds like a perfect plan."

They worked in silence, and after heating up the oil, Declan wondered if he should say something. "Penny for your thoughts?" he asked.

"Just a penny?" Jordan tossed a wink over her shoulder.

He blinked, then sent up a prayer that the heat climbing up his neck didn't reach his cheeks. His beard didn't go high enough to cover them, as it was more like an extended goatee. "How much are thoughts going for these days?"

"Free fish fry."

"Well then, talk away." He turned just as his cheeks warmed.

Sometimes his words felt so rusty around Jordan. Other times he had to keep himself from spilling all his secrets.

"My old roommate called me this morning. It was very…strange."

"How so?"

"First, I have to give you a little backstory." Sizzling filled the air as she talked.

"All right."

"I met my ex at my old job. He came in to buy a gift for his mom."

Declan turned, staring at Jordan's profile. "Where did you work?"

"At a boutique."

"Ah, so he was buying something for another woman."

She whirled around, eyes widening. "What makes you say that?"

"You worked at a boutique. Men don't buy gifts for relatives at those kinds of places." He sure wouldn't.

"Ugh. Where were you when I needed that bit of information?"

"How long did it take you to figure it out?"

"Four months," she groused.

"How did you find out?" Curiosity won out, as the question flew from his lips.

"He accidentally planned a date with all three of us and didn't realize it until we all showed up. That's how we realized our boyfriend was the same boyfriend."

Ouch. "I'm sorry."

"Life, am I right?"

He nodded. "So what did your roommate want?"

Jordan blew out a breath. "To reconcile. She wants to keep our friendship intact."

"Is this the one who's pregnant?" Declan plated one of his fish and one of hers on a dish and added a few hush puppies before handing her the plate. After fixing his meal, he sat at the table. "Should I say grace?"

"Please."

"Thank you for this nourishment, Lord, straight from creation and to the table. Amen."

"Amen. And no, it wasn't the pregnant one who called." Jordan picked up her fork.

Hmm. "Interesting. Maybe the one who called is starting to come to her senses."

"We'll see." Jordan took a bite of her fish.

Declan cut a piece of his, humming softly when it tasted the same as always. Next, he cut off a piece of Jordan's prepared fish and took a bite. Flavor exploded in his mouth. "Wow. You win."

Jordan laughed then wiggled her hands in the air. Declan looked at her across his dinner table. "Jordan?"

"Hmm?" Her gaze left her plate and met his.

"Thank you for making today easier."

She smiled. "You're welcome."

Chapter Ten

"You're awfully quiet this morning," Mike said.

Jordan chewed her bite of breakfast taco, then met her brother's gaze. "I have a lot on my mind."

"Want to talk?"

Did she? She'd managed to evade diving into the subject of her misery yesterday with Declan. Jordan didn't know if he'd even realized that. But the idea of telling her brother, while having a comfort level of knowing each other a long time, also gave her a sense of shame.

"I'm not sure."

Michael peered over his coffee cup as he took a sip. "You know I wouldn't judge you, right, Jay?"

Do I? "You may not mean to, but you might."

Her brother studied her. "I hate that you're probably right. I really need to work on that."

"I know you better than you know yourself." She chuckled but it was forced.

"You have to admit, I'm good at repenting and making up for my gross misjudgments."

Jordan laughed. At Christmastime, he and Vivian had had a falling-out, mostly Michael's fault. To make it up to her, he'd taken her on a carriage ride. They'd been together ever since.

"It did work out, so…" She shrugged.

His lips curved as a faraway look filled his eyes. "I'm so thankful for Vivian." He focused on Jordan. "But I'm also thankful for you. I love you, Pip and Chuck. I want you to know I'm always here for you. It guts me that you felt like you couldn't share your accomplishments."

"I didn't want to fail you."

Mike groaned, dropping his head, his voice low. "I'm not Pop."

"I know that."

"Do you?" His head rose and his gaze met hers. "Do you know you can't fail me? I'm not your father. I'm not your child. I'm your brother. I'll love you no matter what. I don't have some kind of test for you to pass or fail."

Jordan's eyes watered. "Yeah, but it took me forever to get a degree, and you had one by the time you were twenty-two."

"Are you dead?"

She jolted. "No." What was he getting at?

"Then it didn't take you forever." A smug smile turned up his lips.

So, maybe that had been an exaggeration. Still… "I want you to be proud of me."

"Of course I am. You're talented, kind and my sister. Why wouldn't I be proud?"

"Then why won't you let me change the general store around? Why don't you trust me?" The words tore from her throat.

Once again, she found herself in a situation where she wanted to grab the words and stuff them right back in the part of her that stewed over them, examined them over and over until her mind was exhausted. Once her thoughts became voiced, she no longer had control. Now she'd have no choice but to wait and hear what Michael thought. The time of creating different scenarios in her head was over.

Her stomach churned up acid.

"Is that what you think?" Michael sank back into his chair.

Might as well be honest now. She nodded, holding her breath.

Michael rubbed his beard. "I must be a terrible big brother for you to believe I don't trust you."

"No, you're not." The words were automatic and sure.

"I am if you feel like you've failed me. If

you feel I don't trust you." He sighed, rubbing his eyes. "About the store, part of me feels the changes would erase all the memories Pop created and essentially erase him. That's why I've blocked your suggestions every time you ask." Mike's eyes teared up. "I just don't know how to let him go. But I never meant for you to feel like I thought you were incapable of making those improvements."

Her eyes watered once more. *What was wrong with her?* She never cried openly. That was for the shower, where there were no witnesses that life could kick her down and cut through her usual thick skin. "I miss him too."

Mike's Adam's apple bobbed. "Yeah," he choked out. He turned his head.

Probably hiding evidence of his emotions. "I'm sorry I didn't understand that before."

"Don't be. That's my fault for not saying so in the first place." He reached across the table and squeezed her hand, then cleared his throat. "Do you want to share what was bothering you?"

Jordan lifted a shoulder. "Eryn called. She wants to reconcile."

"Oh." Michael nodded slowly. "How do you feel about that?"

"Like I want to ignore her request. I never imagined they would be okay with something like that." After telling Declan about her ex cheating on her, Jordan had come clean to Mike. He'd been shocked but was ready to comfort her or drive to Fayetteville if she needed. Who knew divulging secrets to Declan would make it easier to tell her own brother?

"I'll pray God guides you."

"Thanks, Mike." She smiled and stood.

"What's on your agenda today?"

She placed her plate in the sink. "Declan's bringing the kayaks."

"Awesome. Do you think we'll have a lot of people wanting to rent them?"

"I do." She ran a hand over the top of her head. "People love to go outdoors around here. But not everyone has the money to own a kayak. Providing the rentals will meet their needs."

Mike nodded. "And how are his other items selling?"

"I've had to restock the shelves for the first aid kits. The other items are selling a little bit slower. However, the renters that checked in yesterday bought a couple of hiking items. I gave them one of Declan's brochures." He'd texted her a thanks because they'd booked a guided experience with him that same day.

"Smart idea." Mike rose, taking his dish to the sink. He leaned against the counter. "If you could make one change in the store, what would it be?"

She straightened. "Just one?"

He nodded, wariness creeping into his eyes. Only now she knew what caused that hesitation. She peered up at the ceiling, recalling all her lists and ideas to help the general store. The desire to carry more specialized food for those with specific dietary needs. Or even the idea of moving more items online to expand their reach. If she could only do one thing on her list, what would it be?

"I'd stop selling the items that have little or no consumption. We stock a few items that people never buy. It's like we're just dusting them to look good on the shelf."

He winced. "I take it they're nonperishable items."

"For the most part. The perishable items we don't sell get donated to the food pantry."

Mike nodded. "Do you think the canned items just sit on the shelves at the food pantry as well?"

Jordan didn't know, but it would be nice to at least stop treating them like knickknacks on their own store shelves. She shrugged.

"Okay." He straightened. "Go ahead and make that change."

"Really?" Her heart pounded. Was he really going to trust her with this?

"Really. It needs to be done. I'm sure it'll help our finances in the long run."

She nodded vigorously, imagining River doing the same thing. How she missed that little guy. "It will. Promise."

"I trust you, Jay." He smiled. "Gonna go work on the new places. See you at lunch."

"You're not having it with Vivian?"

He shook his head. "Not today. Today I thought I'd take you and Chuck out."

Why did she keep wanting to shed tears? "Sounds like the perfect plan."

Spending time with her people versus alone? *Yes, please.*

Her mind briefly drifted to Declan. How was he handling solitude? Did he get to talk to River every day? For a brief moment, the desire to text him and ask came upon her. But they didn't have that type of relationship. *Did they?* Besides, she'd see him whenever he showed up today. She'd just have to be patient and ask him then.

Of course, she was concerned about River as well. She prayed he was enjoying his time with his mom. What she wouldn't do to have a little bit more time with hers. She sighed and headed downstairs. *Lord, please bless Declan and River. I pray his ex-wife is cherishing her time with that sweet boy. He's so special and deserves all the love.*

Jordan wiped her face. At least she'd had the

good sense to not put on makeup this morning. If the past hour was any indication, she'd be crying all day.

Trailer hitched to the vehicle, Declan opened the driver's door to hop in, but the sound of a car had him pausing. Their neighborhood rarely had traffic, and hearing another vehicle always caught his attention. He blinked, stunned when Mekayla's vehicle pulled to a stop at the curb. The back door opened, and River jumped out, running at full speed. Declan moved to meet him, swooping up his son and holding him close.

"Dad!" River squeezed his neck tight.

Instinctively, Declan began rubbing soothing circles on his back. "You okay, bud?"

"Now I am."

Declan peered over River's head and met Mekayla's stormy gaze. *Uh-oh.* Declan tugged on his son until River pulled back. Declan stared into his son's light brown eyes, the same color as his mom's. "Hey, can you wait in the Jeep for me? I'm going to talk to your mom."

"Okay." He wiggled, and Declan set him on his two feet.

Once River climbed into his car seat, Declan walked toward Mekayla. "What happened?" he asked quietly. Something had to have gone wrong in order to cut their trip three days short, not that he'd complain.

She crossed her arms, glancing away, lower lip trembling. "He doesn't want me."

Declan tried to keep his frustration to himself. "It's not that," he stated calmly. "River doesn't know you that well. But that will change now that you're visiting him." *Please, let it change.*

As much as he hated sharing River with the woman who left them—knowing River was so far away if he needed Declan—he *knew* his son needed his mother in his life.

Mekayla's tearstained face turned his way. "I can't do this, Dec."

His stomach clenched. "What do you mean?" Each word was enunciated slowly as dread filled his gut.

"I mean…" Her voice trailed off. Then she lifted her chin and met his gaze head on. "I can't be his mother. I have a new life to consider." She rubbed her stomach.

"What about River?" Did she really have no clue she was already a mother? Was she just going to abandon their firstborn?

"He has you."

Declan staggered back. "What did you say to him?" He managed the question through a clenched jaw.

"Only that I was taking him home early. He

cheered." Her lips quirked into a smile, but her eyes were vacant. They looked lifeless.

He rubbed the back of his neck. "Look, I get it. You're probably feeling a little overwhelmed. It's hard being a parent." Especially on days when River threw a fit because there was no PB&J to eat, or the blue cup was dirty and he had to drink out of a red one. But you couldn't quit being a parent. He kept his thoughts to himself, searching for a grace-filled response.

"Mekayla, how about you take a break? Don't make any decisions right now. Just take a breather and call me in a few days."

"The decision has already been made. Hawk completely agrees, as he wants to focus on our family."

What about River? The shout reverberating in Declan's head remained internal.

"He also wanted me to check with you about the money. Can you pay me back yet?"

Right about now, Declan had half a mind to march to a courtroom and file for child support. Maybe then the judge would also agree that he wouldn't have to pay Mekayla. Not when she had gone four years without contributing a single thing to River's upbringing. Only he had no clue if getting the courts involved would further alienate her. Deep down, Declan expected her to change, to put someone else first for once—specifically, their son. If he demanded child support, would she take that as a sign not to show up in person?

Declan blew out a breath and asked for God's strength. "Not yet. I'm waiting on some info from my bank."

"You have four months to get it to me." She flipped her hair behind her back. "I want it before this little one is born."

He just stared at her. There were absolutely no words for what was going on in his mind right now. *None*. Wait… "Aren't you going to say goodbye to River?"

"No. I'm good. Please come get his stuff out of the trunk."

Declan stormed to her car, yanked out the duffel he'd used to pack River's stuff and stomped back to his Jeep. He didn't spare another glance toward Mekayla or say goodbye.

Before he got back in his Jeep, he took a moment to calm himself. It would do no good to slam his door when he hopped into the driver's seat. He had to put on a brave face even though his insides felt like they were crumbling with heartache.

"Dad, I'm so glad you're back."

Declan turned in his seat, grinning at River. "You mean, *I'm* so glad *you're* back."

"That's what I said."

"Yeah, but you were away, not me."

He giggled. "Oh yeah. I'm glad I'm home."

"I am too, bud."

"Where are we going?" River tilted his head, a look of expectancy on his small face.

"To the store."

"Are you going to see Ms. Jordan?"

"Mm-hmm." Declan put the car in Drive and happily listened to River talk all the way to the general store.

Declan was all too happy to hear the silence being chased away. Every day his son had been gone had been a struggle. Maybe it was time Declan took Jordan's advice. He needed to find some friends and get involved with the community. He had the time to do so since he didn't plan on dating anytime soon.

Maybe after River graduates.

An image of Jordan popped into his head, and he chased it away. She wasn't in his plans. He would do well to remember that.

Once he pulled into the general store parking lot, Declan stared at his son through the rearview mirror. "Hey, bud. Wait until I open the door." He could still imagine Mekayla barely coming to a stop before River propelled himself out the back.

When Declan opened the passenger door, River asked, "What are we getting, Dad?"

"Actually, I'm dropping off those kayaks." He pointed toward the trailer.

River's eyes grew wide. "Awesome," he whispered.

They went inside, and Jordan smiled from behind the counter. "River, you're back."

The boy puffed out his chest. "I am. I was gone forever. Nelson was scared at first, but I told him to be brave."

Way to crush my heart. Declan rubbed the back of his neck.

Jordan must have felt the same way, because she laid a hand on her chest. She came out from behind the counter and said, "Aww. I'm so glad you were there for Nelson."

"Me too," River said. He pointed to the stuffed animals. "Can I play with those?"

"May I," Declan muttered.

"May I play with those?" River peered up at him with an expression that said, *Is that better?*

Declan squeezed his shoulder right as Jordan said, "If it's okay with your dad."

"Go ahead, bud."

"You have the kayaks?" Jordan asked, pointing outside.

"And the rack."

"Great. If you want to get it set up on the front porch, I'll do the rest of the work."

"What work?" Was there something he was forgetting?

"Paperwork for rentals, and I have a sign to put out there."

He nodded. "Got it. I'll leave River in here for a little bit, if that's okay?"

She waved him on. "No worries."

How could someone not even related to River have more concern for him than his biological mother? Declan pondered the question as he set to work getting the kayaks displayed. Yet he had come to no conclusion when he walked back into the general store.

He froze at the sight in front of him. Jordan was kneeling before River, making animal noises with the stuffed animals while his son giggled in delight. Frustration, hot and swift, coursed through him. Why couldn't Mekayla have done the same thing? Found some way to bond with her own son? What made it so difficult for her to connect with him?

Declan rubbed the back of his head, breathing out slowly to try to calm down. It wouldn't help anything to get upset. Mekayla had made another exit from their lives, and he'd have to pick up the pieces once more. He could only thank God that River didn't appear to be hurting right now. Declan would have to make sure to talk with him and ensure he was handling everything okay.

Until then, he'd watch Jordan make his son laugh. At least someone else cared besides Declan. Jordan made a silly noise and River fell on the floor, peals of laughter filling the air. Declan gulped. This is what a family should look like. How could he shelve the idea of dating if this could be reality?

Slow down. You're upset. Don't give in to any more feelings toward Jordan. Remember how hurt you were when Mekayla left? Falling for Jordan could leave you more scarred.

Even though Declan could admit that she was a step up—by leaps and bounds—from Mekayla, he didn't want to be so obtuse or imagine that anything could happen between them. She hadn't lived in Willow Springs in years. What was keeping her here? She'd already mentioned that Porter Adventures was a guinea pig so she could do bigger and greater things.

Surely, she didn't mean in Willow Springs.

Declan needed to stick to his no-dating plan. To combat the loneliness and yearning for a complete family, he could find some friends—*male* friends. Friendship was a lot easier and less complicated than adding dating into the mix.

"Hey, bud, let's head back home."

River sat up. "Already?"

Declan glanced at Jordan, seeing the question in her eyes, then shifted his gaze back to his son. "Yeah. We need to unpack."

A paltry excuse, but one that would get him out of the store and into safer territory. Judging from the surprise on Jordan's face, he might have been a little too abrupt. But self-preservation had kicked in.

He maintained his silence as he led River out of the store. Maybe he'd send an email thanking Jordan for all her help or something. They were business associates, after all. *But nothing more. Don't forget that.*

Yet something told him it was too late to put Jordan in that box.

Chapter Eleven

Jordan had lost all leave of her senses. There she stood with a box of muffins—fresh from the Sassy Spoon—ready to knock on Declan's door. Instead of relaxing in bed on her day off, she'd come to see if he was okay and to find out why River had returned early. She'd debated with herself all yesterday as she wondered what happened.

Every time the door chimed with a new customer at the general store and it wasn't Declan, Jordan had grown increasingly moody. Mike had given her a wide berth at home later that evening, choosing to hang out with Vivian because he couldn't take Jordan's mood anymore—his words, not hers.

Yet she couldn't explain why she was so upset. Mike didn't know about Declan's relationship with his ex, and she couldn't imagine

Declan would be okay with her sharing that information without his go ahead. So, this morning, she'd capitulated to that little voice in her head. The one that gave her all the reasons why showing up at his home this morning wasn't a breach of a working relationship but a helping hand for a single dad and his son.

She'd picked up poppy seed muffins from Ma Spooner then driven out to Declan's house. Now if she could only knock on the door instead of second-guessing herself once more. Jordan shifted her feet, staring at the simple doorbell affixed to the doorframe.

What if Declan told her it was none of her business? Of course, she couldn't fault him if he did. Whatever went down with River and his mother was none of Jordan's business. But River had seemed to be suppressing some kind of emotion when playing with the stuffed animals the other day, and Declan looked equal parts relieved and frustrated. Not to mention the strange way they'd left so quickly. The radio silence was killing her.

Somehow, some way, Jordan had come to care for the Porter men. Just in a loving-thy-neighbor way, being part of the kingdom and all that good stuff.

Right, Jay. Keep telling yourself that.

Before her thoughts continued to spiral as she

deliberated on whether or not knocking was a smart idea, the door flew open. She gasped, taking a step back.

Declan leaned against the frame, folded his arms and smirked. "Good morning."

"Morning," she squeaked. Jordan cleared her throat, ignoring the flames heating her cheeks.

"You've been standing out here for about ten minutes now. When I first spotted you, you'd just stepped onto the porch. I figured I'd wait. A couple of minutes went by, and I noticed you had something in your hand." He pointed to the box. "Once I figured out that's a Sassy Spoon takeout box, my curiosity shot through the roof."

She smiled, loving the flow of words coming from him. "So you decided to open the door now?"

"Yes. I'm hungry and can't wait any longer for you to finish talking to yourself." He narrowed his eyes in scrutiny. "That was what you were doing, right?"

"Sadly, yes." How mortifying to know he'd seen her waffling.

"Would you like to come in, or should I take the box and leave you to your thoughts?"

Jordan laughed. "Yes, I'd like to come in. Please."

Declan stepped back, motioning her forward. Jordan gave an inward shake of the head, pleased by his friendliness, but a little bit shocked as well. Was he happy to see her? And why did that thought spread warmth throughout her heart?

"What's in the container?" He eyed the box in her hand.

"Poppy seed muffins," she replied.

His head fell back, a low groan tumbling from him. "The Spooners makes the *best* food."

"Agreed." She glanced around the home, noticing the stillness. "River still asleep?" Was she that early?

"Yeah. He's been having a rough time falling asleep."

She studied Declan. "Is he really, or are you just so happy to have him home you've been letting him stay up late?"

His lips quirked. "Maybe that last one." He got a plate from the cabinet, placed a muffin on top, then slid it into the microwave.

"What are you doing?" She stared, horrified.

"Uh." Declan turned and faced her, the microwave heating up the muffin. "The obvious." He hooked a thumb over his shoulder. "Warming my muffin up."

"But I just brought it from the diner."

"Then proceeded to stand on my front stoop for ten minutes. The heat might have seeped out."

Jordan laughed. "You've got a point." She

gestured to the dining table. "Mind if I take a seat?"

"Sure. Want some coffee?"

"If you have some already made."

"I don't, but it won't take that long to make a pot. Plus, how can you eat a muffin without liquid sustenance?"

"Wow. You're in a mood." Why was he so captivating today? *Stop that line of thought, missy.*

"Just happy River's back."

Now was the time to share the reason for her visit. But when he turned his warm blue eyes her way, Jordan's breath hitched, and the words got stuck in her throat.

"It was so quiet without him. He must have talked all day when he got back and continued the next day. I haven't had the heart to shush him or make him go to bed on time."

"It is spring break, after all," Jordan said quietly.

"Right. Now that it's Saturday, I suppose I'll have to get him back on schedule in time for school Monday."

He took his muffin out of the microwave and gestured to the box. "Want me to heat you one up?"

"I'll eat mine from the box." She made a show of taking a huge bite. "Still warm."

Declan chuckled then tasted his own muffin. "Perfect temperature and best tasting muffin ever," he mumbled.

Jordan held up a napkin. "Stop spraying crumbs. Manners, please."

His lips curved upward, but his mouth kept chewing as he took bite after bite. When Declan was done, he said, "I appreciate the breakfast."

"You're welcome."

He got up and poured coffee into two mugs. "Do you need cream or sugar?"

"Yes to both." What good was coffee plain?

Peeking in the fridge, Declan said, "I have vanilla creamer and half and half. Which one would you like?"

"Vanilla please."

He handed her the creamer. After she doctored up her coffee, she took a sip. The small talk, eating muffins and drinking coffee did nothing to silence her thoughts. The words she wanted to say kept dancing around in her mind. But how should she broach the subject that brought her to Declan's doorstep this morning?

"So what brought you by?" Declan eyed her over his coffee cup.

"Um." He was just going to rip the bandage, huh? "Well, I was wondering about River. He came home early, huh?"

Declan set his mug down. "Yeah." His voice sounded grave.

Goose bumps broke out along Jordan's arms. "What happened?" she asked softly.

"Mekayla decided she couldn't handle being his mother and that it was better that she devote time to her new family."

Jordan shook her head. "I'm sorry, say that again?" She couldn't have possibly heard him correctly.

Who wouldn't want to be around River and soak up all the wonderful things that made him *him*? And what new family was Declan talking about?

Declan dragged a hand down his face.

He never imagined Jordan would show up on his front steps with breakfast and get him to spill his guts. But that's exactly what she was asking of him right now. Strangely, he found that he wanted to share.

"My ex dropped River off the other day practically in tears." He leaned forward, letting his coffee mug warm his hands. "I honestly don't know if it was her belief that River didn't want to be around her or the fact that she's expecting."

Jordan's eyes bugged out.

Declan nodded. "Yep. By the time our conversation was over, she wore an odd smile and proclaimed her new life deserved all her attention." He snorted. "Apparently, her new husband agrees with the plan."

"I'm sorry, but what did you *ever* see in her?"

His mind turned Jordan's words over, trying to recall what had attracted him to Mekayla in the first place. "You know, I'm not really sure. I've asked myself that countless times. Mostly at the beginning of our divorce, and then again when she dropped off River and essentially told me she'd never see him again."

A wave of frustration hit him as he recalled his desperation to get her to see reason. How, when he called her yesterday, the phone went straight to voicemail. Was she going to ignore them forever? The thought had only intensified the gutted feeling that had yet to leave Declan's heart.

"Does River understand what's going on?" Jordan laid a hand on the table, eyes widening in earnest.

"I tried to bridge the conversation with him. Asked him if he had fun with his mom as a starter." He rubbed his head. "I tried to feel out what he was thinking."

"What did he say?" Jordan whispered.

Declan swallowed, remembering River's matter-of-fact response. "Told me that Mekayla didn't like him and that it was okay because he knew I loved him. As long as he didn't have to visit her again, he'd be happy."

Jordan's eyes watered. "That's awful."

"It really is. But what's worse—" he blew out a breath "—is that River seems completely fine. I want to ask more questions, but will that only make him feel bad when he truly seems okay?" Declan wanted to throw up his hands and give in to an adult-size tantrum. Life really wasn't fair.

"Ugh, how are you supposed to know which direction to go?" Jordan propped her chin on her hand.

"When I figure that out, I'll let you know."

"Ha." She sighed. "It was killing me, you know."

"Not knowing what was going on in *my* life?" He arched an eyebrow and curved his mouth to let her know he was only joking—or rather, hid the fact that he was touched.

She cared enough to stop by with breakfast and check on his son. Something River's own mother couldn't be bothered with. If Declan had any guts, he'd tell Jordan just how dangerous her concern was to his peace of mind. How could he maintain his defenses when she was dissolving them with so much kindness?

"Yes! You were so morose when River left to

visit his mom. Looked like someone kicked you in the stomach and left you to suffer." She poked out her bottom lip. "Then a few days later, you show up with him in tow, and he was *beaming*, by the way. It was a complete one-eighty and had my mind spinning." She shook her head, as if mimicking the spiraling events. "I had so many questions, but you refused to come back into the store."

"You could have called or texted, you know."

She stilled. "Really? Do we have that type of…friendship, that I can check on you and get a real response?"

The hint of vulnerability shining in Jordan's eyes made something that felt very much like the need to protect rise up in him. *Ugh, Porter. You aren't supposed to think of her like that.*

But it was too late. Jordan had him thinking all sorts of *what-ifs*. Made him question his plan to maintain their business relationship and nothing else. Only now that she mentioned friendship, Declan knew he could use another one.

"Yes, Jordan. We're close enough friends that I'll tell you the truth." He forced an easy grin. "Besides, you've already heard way too much of my personal story."

"Likewise," she quipped. She grabbed a piece of her muffin, holding the small chunk. "Thank you for telling me, by the way," Jordan continued. "You didn't have to."

"Guess I needed to share with someone and get it off my chest." He really did feel a little better having shared his frustrations. "Besides, I couldn't talk about it before."

"So why now?"

"You bribed me with food." He grabbed another muffin and popped it into the microwave. Once it beeped, he sat back down.

"I'm glad that idea woke me up in the middle of the night, then." She studied him. "How can I pray for you? For River?"

Declan froze, his arm holding the muffin in midair. "You want to pray for me? I mean 'us'?" When had someone other than church acquaintances asked to pray for him? The gesture seemed to heal the cracks in his veneer.

"I mean, I know you said River seems fine, but is he really? Are *you*?"

Am I? If she'd asked right after Mekayla's visit, Declan would've given an emphatic no. But now, time had erased some of his frustration. The selfish part of him cheered over the fact he wouldn't have to share his son while the other half mourned the loss of River having his mother. He wouldn't wish a motherless childhood on anyone, let alone his son.

"I don't know," he answered.

Jordan studied him. "That makes sense."

"Does it? It doesn't to me." He'd prayed to God. Shared all his thoughts and feelings about the whole situation. Yet he hadn't felt any resolution afterward, though his anxiety had dropped a notch. That was something, at least.

"That's because this isn't a black-and-white situation. You're probably wrestling with guilt over being happy he's home safe, against the idea that your ex wants nothing more to do with him." Jordan sighed. "It would definitely make me feel some kind of way."

Declan nodded at the expression. "Ain't that the truth?" He definitely felt some kind of way, he just couldn't quite put a word to the emotion. He sipped his coffee. "I haven't talked this much in a while."

"You don't say." She smirked.

"It's true." He nodded sagely. "River does all the talking most of the day. The only time I get to carry on a conversation is on a guided tour. Even then, I'm sure to leave enough silence so the tourists can enjoy nature."

Her dark brown eyes assessed him. "What makes you talk to me, then? Is it my nosy nature or my winsome charm?"

A bark of laughter escaped from his lips. "Probably that nosy nature."

Her shoulders shook with laughter while her

eyes danced with mirth, but not a sound escaped.

What would make her crack and let the joy fly free? "It also might be that I've been thinking of you as my own personal shrink."

Her eyes widened and something flitted through. Something undefinable, but Declan continued the charade. "I picture lying in a kayak, completely at ease. And you're on a paddle board asking me, 'How does that make you feel?'"

Jordan's bellow of laugher almost shocked Declan, but he'd been waiting for something to let loose. Soon, he joined in, thankful for a moment of fun after such a hard few days. He drew in some deep breaths to calm down, then spied River padding on bare feet toward them. A curious light covered his face as his eyes roamed back and forth between Declan and Jordan.

"Morning, bud." Declan held out an arm to pull his son in for a hug. He pressed a kiss to his forehead. "Have a good sleep?"

River nodded. "Hi, Ms. Jordan."

"Good morning, River. Want a muffin?" Her gaze switched to Declan's, asking if it was okay.

He dipped his head.

"Yes, ma'am. Will you warm it up?"

She froze, then bore a stare right into Declan's soul.

He held up his hands. "I can't help it if the kid knows how to eat a muffin right."

She muttered, "More like you brainwashed him."

Declan chuckled.

"When did Ms. Jordan get here, Dad? How come you didn't wake me? Are we going to do something today?" River finally took a breath.

Declan jumped in before his son could ask another load of questions he didn't have answers to. "She got here about thirty minutes ago. And I wanted you to rest."

"Y'all going somewhere?" Jordan asked, setting a plate before River.

"Let's do something together," River cheered.

Jordan appeared startled for a moment before she looked at Declan, a curious expression in her eyes. "What do you think of that?" she asked.

"I, uh…" He ran a hand through his hair.

What did he think? Going out together would surely lead to a treacherous path. It might set an expectation that he saw Jordan in a more-than-friendly light. He couldn't bring another woman into River's life, especially after what happened with Mekayla. It would be better to reassure River that Declan would always be here for him, and no one would ever get in the way of that.

"I think we should hang out by ourselves,

bud." Declan tossed him a smile. "Maybe we could go fishing." He gazed at River, ignoring the heat of Jordan's gaze.

Besides, maybe she was relieved she wouldn't have to bond with the Porter men. But if she wasn't, Declan definitely didn't want to read any of that emotion in her gaze.

"But I want Ms. Jordan to come," River whined.

An ache filled Declan's chest. "It's her day off. Maybe she has plans already."

River swung his head toward her. "Do you? Will you go fishing with us? Pretty please?" He clasped his hands under his chin, wide-eyed gaze directed at her.

Declan's stomach dropped. No way she could say no now, and no way he could make her. Slowly, he directed his stare her way and gave a simple nod.

She studied Declan, then smiled at his son. "I'd love to, River."

"Yay!" he cheered.

Declan wanted to drop his head into his hands but let a soft smile cover his lips instead. No use crying over spilled milk when he had paper towels. Only he had no idea what the paper towels were in this situation.

Chapter Twelve

Instead of buying poppy seed muffins from the Sassy Spoon, Jordan should've sat down and listed reasons why poking one's nose in other people's business could go so very wrong. Like how she'd found herself back in waders; only this time, River accompanied her and Declan. She couldn't help but think they made a picture of a cute family.

Which was why she should have kept to herself and ignored the mystery of River's return. Now she had to battle against all the feelings and reasons why being with a single dad was an extra complication she didn't want.

Jordan blew out a breath, staring into the water. *Lord God, how did I get so off track?* Somehow she'd let her desire to prove she could turn Declan's business around cause her to drop her guard. She'd stopped being wary of him as a man and a potential person to hurt or disappoint her. Without meaning to, she'd come to care about the things that mattered to the Porter men.

That was so not a good thing. She needed to retreat, regroup and hopefully return to her original plan. Work on getting more traffic to Declan's website with the hopes online searchers would turn into real-life customers. Not to mention ensuring that his goods sold well at the general store.

Actually, the kayaks had been seeing a lot of rentals since the weather continued to warm up this spring. A lot of the hiking gear Declan had ordered was selling well too, either to locals or tourists. The added business, plus ridding the store of the never-sold products, meant Michael was beginning to notice the odd layout of the remaining items. Hopefully, he'd give her the okay to change things around soon.

Which meant her business dreams were going according to plan. Michael was finally taking her seriously while Declan's business was headed toward the goals he'd outlined. Life was looking up. Jordan needed to get it through her head that the outlook didn't necessarily mean she could let her guard down with men.

If she had to pick at the scab that was her ex and remind herself why entering the dating fray would land her right back in the failure category, she would. Making the decision to forgive Traun and her two ex-friends didn't mean that Jordan wanted to admit that there were good men in the world.

Please, you already think that about Declan.

She squeezed her eyes tight. Of course she did. Who cared if the what-ifs were louder than the *guard your heart* cautionary whispers in her head? Just because Declan was attractive, faithful to the Lord and a godly man for his son to look up to didn't mean Jordan had to take a romantic interest in him. But goodness it was hard not to think about Declan and whether he was good boyfriend material.

What if he could actually be interested in her? What if they could be a couple? What if they fit better than she had with any man she'd dated? And what if he was *the one*?

What an utterly ridiculous notion, considering how much grief he'd given her when he first walked into the general store a few weeks ago asking for Mike as if she were nonexistent. The annoyance that had filled her, the snark that came out of her mouth, should be reason enough why they would never work. It didn't matter that she'd gotten to know him better and understood that his aloofness was not necessarily a rebuke. Still, Jordan would continue to assure herself that Declan Porter could never be interested in her. Anything to keep her from thinking of more *what-ifs*.

He was a single dad with a complicated past. He had his own failed relationships to dwell on. Surely that, his son and his business occupied his mind, keeping romantic relationship thoughts at bay. All of those reasons were why Jordan needed to run the other way. Avoiding baby mama drama was high on her list. Of course, his ex seemed to have exited stage left, abandoning River once more.

She glanced toward her right, watching River. He seemed unaffected by the absence of his mom, and that made her heart ache even more for the Porter men. She straightened her spine.

Lord, please help me remember the pain of Traun's betrayal. I can't open myself up back to that level of hurt. She gulped. If she allowed herself to fall for Declan, her world could very well be ripped apart. Something told her that if she let herself love him, her heart would be engaged to the fullest. Whatever emotion she thought she'd felt toward Traun would pale in comparison. Not to mention the kind of damage it would inflict on her business goals. How could she focus on them if she was mooning over Declan Porter?

You need to remember to seek your purpose in life, Jay. To seek God and not your own desires.

Wait? Was she saying that being with Declan was something she wanted? That couldn't be right, could it?

"I'm hungry, Dad." River's voice broke the silence.

Jordan expelled a breath she hadn't been aware she'd been holding. She set her pole in the holder, then walked toward him. "I'll help you with lunch."

"Thanks, Ms. Jordan."

"Thanks, Jordan," Declan added softly with a small smile.

She would ignore the goose bumps his voice elicited and focus on River's adorable self. She ruffled his curls and almost let out a sigh when he wrapped his small arms around her waist. "I'm happy to help."

Shame on Declan's ex for leaving this precious boy. River had firmly entrenched himself in Jordan's heart so swiftly. How could Mekayla be immune to the love pouring from this child?

River pulled away, grabbing Jordan's hand to drag her toward the riverbank. She blinked rapidly against the rising tears as she thought over his predicament. Tilting her head up and backward was certainly no help.

As the tug on her hand propelled her forward once more, Jordan's foot caught a rock. Instinctively she dropped River's hand to ensure she wouldn't fall on him. Her body surged forward, and her arms flew out to catch her. Only the ground never finished rushing toward her face. Instead, strong arms wrapped around her waist and tugged her up.

"You okay?" Declan's low tenor sent flutters through her middle.

Not if you keep holding me. She stepped out of his arms. "Mm-hmm." If she spoke, she'd probably squeak, and that would be all too embarrassing. Still, she had to thank him, right? "Nice save. The rocks would've pulverized me." *Keep it cool, just keep it cool.* But her cheeks were feverish as her heart pounded in her chest.

"Most likely."

Declan sounded so serious. Her gaze immediately shifted to his, only to see a mischievous grin curving his lips. She quickly averted her eyes so she wouldn't be tempted to ask if he could ever look at her lovingly. At least, she had enough sense to keep her mouth shut as she worked through her conflicting emotions.

She knelt down and grabbed some moist towelettes to clean her hands, then River's, so they could eat. Next, she took out the food Declan had packed for them.

"Do you need help?" Declan asked.

Jordan's back stiffened. His voice sounded way too close. "I got it."

"Okay. I'll set the blanket down, so we have somewhere to sit."

She nodded, keeping her gaze where it was safe.

"I want to help, Ms. Jordan."

She peered up at River. "Take those containers to your dad." How many could she actually expect him to carry at his age? "But carry them one at a time." That should be easy, right?

"Okay."

After unpacking everything, Jordan reached for the plates. They weren't plastic or paper, but ones used for camping. Jordan worked on autopilot before coming to sit on the blanket with Declan and River.

"We should do this every day." River threw his arms wide, half-eaten PB&J in his hand.

"What about school?" Jordan asked, ignoring the part of her that wanted the same thing.

"Okay, *after* school." River smiled, then took a bite of his sandwich.

"Ms. Jordan works, River, remember?"

"Not all day though." His gaze turned from his dad to Jordan. "Right?"

"Right." She swallowed around a lump in her throat.

"See, Dad? We could do this every day like a real family."

Jordan's gaze locked onto Declan's. Her

breath hitched as River's thought echoed her what-ifs from moments ago. Declan's eyes darkened with intensity. What was he thinking? Did he have the same hopes and dreams as his son, or did he only see her as the bossy woman who had to get her own way?

She broke the locked stare. "Are you done? Should I clean up?" she asked to no one in particular. Why couldn't she get her heart rate back down?

"We'll do it, right, River?" Declan said.

"Right."

They soon packed up to return back home. By then, Jordan was practically crawling out of her skin and ready to bolt out of the car as soon as it came to a stop. Today's trip had her thinking of dreams she hadn't imagined since dating Traun. Only time told her somehow with Declan it would be all too different. But was that different good or bad?

She managed to keep a calm facade for River's sake. She laughed at his jokes, paid attention when he talked to her and gave him a hug goodbye. She waved then hightailed it to her car.

As she shut the door—also shutting out the world—Jordan let out a breath, head against the steering wheel. "What just happened, Lord?" she whispered in the confines of her car.

* * *

Declan shut the door quietly behind him, then leaned his head against the frame. Now that River was in bed, Declan could grab a seat on his deck and talk with the Lord. Today had been one of the strangest days he'd experienced in a while. And considering the complexities with Mekayla, that was saying something.

This thing between him and Jordan was starting to feel like the emotions weren't all one-sided. When River had suggested they could be a real family, Declan had been captivated by Jordan's deep brown eyes and had wanted to close the gap between them. Yet he couldn't forget the ups and downs he'd experienced lately. The drama Mekayla had brought into his life. Not to mention his own plans of not dating.

Being abandoned, whether unintentionally—God rest his grandma's soul—or intentionally (that was, Mekayla and his own mother) had done a number on Declan's trust and desire to put his heart on the line. Jordan made him wonder if taking another chance would yield better results that would come with lifelong devotion and happiness.

Even though Jordan brought her own drama with her fiery nature, it wasn't the chaotic kind that made him want to retreat into quiet. It was more entertaining than anything and made

Declan loosen up in a way he didn't normally. However, seeing how attached River was becoming was enough for Declan to keep the distance. Or at least, when his son wasn't using those big brown eyes to get what he wanted, like a fishing excursion.

Declan didn't want his son getting confused and thinking Jordan's presence meant more than business. He needed to put a stop to any more outings that would be just the three of them. Because if he allowed River to become dependent on Jordan's presence—and if Declan let himself fall for her—it would be all the more devastating when she decided Willow Springs was no longer for her.

He had no intention of ever leaving this town again. This community, these people, were it for him. Since Porter Adventures was beginning to get more reservations, Declan was ready to erase his backup plan of entering the work force with a nine-to-five job. All he had to do was make a call to the bank Monday to ensure the loan would be approved, allowing him to close the last chapter on him and Mekayla.

He and River could use closure from her flitting in and out of their lives. Tonight, when he'd tucked River into bed, his son had asked why his own mom didn't love him. Despite Declan's protest, River didn't believe she truly did. If

Declan told Mekayla about River's thoughts, would she change her mind about not seeing their son again?

Declan dialed her number. After one ring, it went straight to voicemail. Either her phone was dead, or she was still ignoring his calls. He pulled up the text message app and typed one out to her.

Declan: Hey Mekayla. I wanted to ask if you'd reconsider visiting River in the future. I know your first visit might not have gone as expected, but over time, it'll get better. Please don't cut all ties with him.

Mekayla: This is her husband Hawk. Please do not contact her again. We have our own family. You go handle yours.

Declan's jaw clenched. Was this guy serious?

Declan: You do know she has a son already, right?

But he simply stared at the message, the cursor blinking in place, his finger hovering over Send. He dropped his head back, looking up into the night sky. "God, what do I do?"

If she truly wanted nothing to do with River,

what recourse was left to him? He deleted the message, scanned the names listed in his contacts and stopped on Brendan's. He pressed the green icon and placed the phone up to his ear.

"Hello?"

"Hey, Brendan. It's Declan."

"Twice in one month! What's up? Everything okay?"

"Well, uh, not really." Declan swallowed. "I was wondering if there's any way to force visitation."

"For Mekayla? Did something happen?"

Declan caught his friend up to speed. How his ex no longer wanted to visit River and the early return from spring break. "Surely, there's a way to get her to see River. That can't be it, can it?"

Brendan sighed. "Man, I'm sorry, but if she doesn't want to see your son anymore, she doesn't have to. Most courts won't force that. Does she pay child support?"

Heat filled Declan's face. "No."

"Why in the world not?" Shock filled his friend's voice.

"I, uh, never asked for it. Since we went through a mediator to file everything, I thought it best to just end it peacefully." Besides, if she didn't have to pay money, wouldn't it make it easier for her to return to them?

Now the thought felt foolish, but Declan

didn't know how to change years of thinking along those lines.

"Declan, there's peaceful, and then there's no action on your part. You still have the right to take her to court since your son is…how old is he?"

"Five."

"Yeah, she can pay child support until he's eighteen or graduates college, however it gets stipulated. Especially since she's not willing to use her visitation time. At least she can add to his upbringing monetarily."

Declan bounced his foot up and down. "What if I don't want her money?" Money wouldn't make memories between River and Mekayla. Money wouldn't fill the spot of a mother in a boy's life.

If he made waves, he couldn't guarantee that River wouldn't be hurt further in the aftermath. Though the money would be nice, Declan didn't want it if it came with a cost that would hurt his son.

"Why wouldn't you?"

Declan opened his mouth to respond but closed it.

"Is it the reversed roles? Usually, men are the ones paying child support. Is that it? Would it feel odd to receive it from her?"

He blew out a breath. "I want her in River's life. Money doesn't guarantee that."

"Is that why you didn't fight for sole custody? I mean, you should if she's not willing to see your boy or help pay for him."

Declan rubbed his face. "After being served with divorce papers, my initial thought had been shock that it was even happening. Then I realized I wanted to pave a way for her to come back if she changed her mind. Asking for child support at the time seemed counterintuitive." He gulped. "Now I just want her to see her son."

"I get that, man. I really do, but consider this from a logical standpoint. If she doesn't want to help raise her kid, aka use her visitation rights, then she can help pay to take care of him. I'd be happy to file a petition for child support for you, pro bono."

"Yeah?" Declan ran a hand through his hair.

"Yes. It'll be a thank-you for all the times you helped me in class."

Declan laughed. "Question—Mekayla wants me to pay her back the money she gave me to start my business. Could I get that voided in lieu of child support?" If he even decided to go down that path.

"Good question. Tell me more."

So Declan did. He explained how she'd given him four months to pay him back—just in time for her new child to be born. That it was ten thousand he needed to pay back, and how the bank wanted proof he was worth the loan risk. Declan even brought up how Jordan was helping him improve his business. Brendan had some good insight for Declan and asked probing questions. Yet at the end of the conversation, Declan gave the okay for his friend to file for child support and work out a way for Declan to not pay Mekayla back either.

He felt lighter after the conversation. His brain, seeing that part dealt with, jumped right back to his feelings for Jordan. The woman had his mind reeling like a spinning ride at a carnival with no easy exit. Declan was thankful tomorrow was Sunday. Maybe Pastor Liam would deliver a sermon just for him. Declan could use the Lord's wisdom and guidance right about now.

His phone chimed again, this time a text from Michael Wood.

Big Mike: Want to join us for lunch tomorrow after church?

Declan: I don't want to encroach on family time.

More like don't want to see Jordan while I'm trying to put distance between us.

Big Mike: You won't. Vivian will be here, and she invited some of her friends. We'll probably turn it into a barbecue, cookout or something. The more, the merrier.

Declan: I'll think about it.

Big Mike: No pressure.

Oh, but there was. If Declan said yes, it would be just one more opportunity to interact with Jordan and have River become used to her presence. On the other hand, it was an opportunity for Declan to mingle within the community and stop feeling so isolated.

Some days, adulting was the worst.

Chapter Thirteen

When Jordan moved back to Willow Springs, she'd checked off the box on the church form for volunteering. Even though the church had informed her they had enough volunteers, they still did a background check on Jordan. Vivian, who worked as the church secretary, had said it was for just-in-case purposes.

Apparently, today was that day. Seemed a stomach bug was going around town, and the helpers who normally led the kindergarten class were out sick. When Jordan's phone chimed last night with an incoming text asking if she'd be able to assist, she'd texted back that she'd be there bright and early.

Only now that she'd walked into the classroom and discovered her co-volunteer was Declan Porter, Jordan wanted to walk right back out of the room and keep walking until the distance between her and Declan was immeasurable.

His lips wavered in what she *thought* was a smile but looked more like a grimace. Since she probably had the same expression on her face, she wouldn't pass judgment. River held no qualms, however, and ran right up to her, squeezing her legs.

"Good morning. How are you?" She stared into his happy face.

"Great. I love church, and now you and Dad will be teaching us. It's the best day ever!" His enthusiastic cry filled the room.

Her stomach dropped to her toes. "Yes, I need to go talk to your dad about that."

"Okay." River dropped his arms.

Jordan made her feet go one before the other, ignoring the feeling of a death march toward the one guy she'd told herself to avoid. "Hey," she murmured.

Ugh. Why is this so awkward?

Declan dipped his head. "I gather you're helping out today?"

"Yep." Not much more to say than that.

"We, uh, we'll be doing a story, then a craft." Declan slid his hands into his pockets. He looked nice in a green plaid shirt. "Natalie said it was pretty self-explanatory."

At least something was. Surely Jordan could

focus on the kids and ignore the man beside her. *I hope.* "What story are we teaching them?"

"The friendship between Jonathan and David. Do you want to read the story and I'll lead the craft time, or the other way around?" Declan asked, his gaze firmly affixed to the craft sheets on the table.

He hadn't looked at her once, and for some reason, that made Jordan want to cry. The emotion frustrated her, which only added to her mounting despair.

Maybe after class, Jordan should ask Declan how he felt about her. Surely if he thought the idea of them dating laughable, she could shrug off the what-ifs and move forward. Not that she *wanted* to date. Okay, yes, she did. She could admit to herself what she'd been denying for so long.

If Declan didn't feel the same, she would just treat him like any other church acquaintance— after she cried in the shower and ate her feelings.

She swallowed hard. "Um, I can lead the craft if you're comfortable reading."

"Yeah, I can do that." He rubbed the back of his neck.

"Are you really okay reading the story?" She eyed him. "I only suggested that because I figured the craft would be more intensive. That way, you only have to help one or two kids who need it."

His gaze met hers, intensity burning behind them. "I'm good," he assured her.

"Okay. Then I am too," she said softly. *No, I'm not. Do you like me? Could we be a couple?*

Jordan stepped back. What had come over her? She'd thought after the little fishing escapade yesterday that she wanted nothing to do with Declan and River. Hadn't she told herself that nothing could ever happen between them? But with one hug from River and a look that bore into her soul from Declan, she'd caved. She had no choice but to admit what her heart and been whispering to her.

Kids began filing in, and Jordan purposely switched off her thoughts and focused on ensuring all the kids were checked in correctly. After a few minutes had passed and no new kids had entered, Jordan turned away from the door and glanced at the classroom clock.

She clapped her hands together, a few kids turning her way at the sound. "All right, everyone. Let's sit on the carpet so Mr. Porter can read our lesson for the day."

The kids scrambled to the rug, sitting crisscross applesauce. Jordan took a seat on the stool behind them so she could make sure the kids kept their hands to themselves.

When everyone went silent, Declan started reading the lesson. His low voice captivated the kids, and they sat still. Their eyes remained glued to the book he read from. Then one of the kids raised his hand.

"Why are we reading about friends? Doesn't everyone have one?" the little boy asked with a lisp.

Jordan waited to hear what Declan would say.

"Most everyone has a friend," Declan started out slowly. "But you have to remember that someone could be new to your school and not know anyone."

"Ohhh," the class murmured.

"But also, sometimes people don't pick the best friends. Sometimes they worry about not having any friends, so instead, they'll pick someone who's mean to them."

"Like a bully?" a little girl asked.

"That's right. When we look at David and Jonathan, we can learn the characteristics—"

"What's carrot sticks?" River asked.

Jordan tried to contain her laughter, but the pinkened cheeks on Declan's face didn't help matters any.

His Adam's apple bobbed. "Not carrot sticks, River—characteristics," he said, enunciating clearly. "It's the qualities you want in a friend or even common interests that you share. For example, River, you might want a friend who likes dinosaurs."

"Yes." He pumped his arms close to his body.

"Why do you think David and Jonathan decided to be friends?" Jordan asked, offering a lifeline to Declan. He was starting to look a little unnerved.

"Because he was kind," one of the girls said.

"Very good." Jordan smiled. "Anyone else?"

Hands shot up all over the room. For the next fifteen minutes, they talked about what they wanted in a friend. Jordan couldn't help but think of Declan. As much as she had tried to ignore his positive traits in the beginning, her mind had subconsciously cataloged them anyway. How steadfast he was. How he remained patient with River when all those questions being pelted at him had to make him a little irritated. And how he was intent on making his business a success. Declan Porter was no quitter.

All of those traits had started to swarm around Jordan's defenses, and little by little, the wall around her heart had fallen down like Jericho. The reasons she had against dating again all seemed like flimsy excuses. She could actually admit she wasn't nursing a broken heart over Traun. If anything, she was more upset that her best friends had picked him over her.

Jordan shook herself from her thoughts and grabbed the crafts. After placing one in front of each chair lined along the two long tables in the classroom, she called the kids forward. She explained the craft, then she and Declan started assisting the children who raised their hands for help. As predicted, Declan ended up helping at least two of the kids. Their class was old enough that they didn't require a lot of help. A little spelling help here, a glue stick to pull apart there.

She glanced at the time, then instructed the kids to clean up their messes. By the time church was over and parents began to pick up their kids, Jordan was exhausted. She couldn't wait to go home, grab a book or just a cup of coffee, and relax. Maybe talking to Declan could wait until she'd had time to really think about being open to dating. Maybe she'd find a trail to hike through or even go kayaking. *Just me, myself and I.*

"You ready to sign out?" Declan asked.

Jordan turned to see that only the three of them remained in the room. "Yes." She bit her lip. "You go ahead. I'll turn off the lights and whatnot."

Declan nodded. He turned to walk out the door, but her brother appeared in the doorway.

"Great. You're both here."

She arched an eyebrow. "You were looking for the two of us?" The hairs on her neck rose in awareness.

Mike nodded. "Yeah. I invited Declan over for lunch yesterday. Wanted to see if he was coming and if you were ready to go."

Jordan's stomach dropped to her toes. She'd forgotten about the cookout. A quick glance at Declan was enough time to see a look of regret flash in his eyes. Did he not want to hang out with her? Was he upset she'd managed to horn in on his time with River yesterday?

"Uh, Mike, I hadn't decided."

"We should go, Dad. Can we?" River pleaded.

Her heart thumped. How could Declan resist those puppy dog eyes? Declan's gaze flickered from River's to Jordan's, as if asking permission. Not that he needed her permission. Maybe she was reading into everything.

She cleared her throat. "Yeah, we always have plenty of food."

"She's right," Mike added.

When she got in the car later, she would give Mike a lesson on asking a parent a question in front of their kid.

"Then thanks. We'll be over soon," Declan said softly.

Jordan followed Mike out of the room. Did this mean she should just rip the bandage off and ask Declan how he felt when he came over? *Lord, please show me what to do.*

Declan couldn't take the strain anymore. The moment he could find spare time to pull Jordan to the side, he would. As much as he wanted to avoid her, that just wasn't working. Willow Springs didn't have enough square footage for that. Not to mention, every move she made had his senses tuned in, categorizing every detail that made Jordan who she was.

Like the scent that was purely her. It smelled like sunshine and baked goods. Or the fact that her footsteps were always light, but he could still hear the whisper of movement when she walked. Or the way her laugh made others smile and draw closer to her. Of course there was also the fierce loyalty she showed to family and friends, and the determination to see everything through.

Instead of fighting the run-ins around town, he could greet her like he would any friend. As much as the idea of becoming romantically involved piqued his interest, he was a single dad with a business that was barely scraping by. What could he offer her?

Better to be friends so that if they were ever volunteering in the same church classroom with one another again (seriously, what were the odds?) or attended the same lunch, they didn't have to avoid horrific small talk. Talking with Jordan was easy for Declan when they were just business associates or acting friendly. It was the idea of *more* that had him clamming up and avoiding her gaze, afraid she'd read his thoughts.

Just how are you going to make those thoughts go away?

Maybe the intense scrutiny from the eldest Wood sibling would wipe his mind clean. Mike seemed to have figured out some of Declan's thoughts, glancing back and forth between Declan and Jordan as if trying to put the puzzle pieces together. Had Declan's introspective silence tipped him off?

Pippen laughed at one of River's jokes, and Declan tried to focus his attention on the now. He looked around the table in the Woods' home. When he'd first sat down, Declan hadn't been able to tell if being across from Jordan was a good thing or not.

"Have you ever met a dinosaur you haven't liked, River?" Vivian asked. She was situated across from River and next to Jordan.

His son frowned. "Dinosaurs are dead. How can I have met them?"

A bemused expression flitted across Jordan's face. *Why are you watching her, Declan? Pay attention to your son.* But the topic had already been changed as River rattled off the different ways to fish in Arkansas.

"You should go with us one day," his son added. "Ms. Jordan has, and we had lots of fun."

"Is that right?" Big Mike asked.

He'd taken the spot of head of the household, sitting at the end of the table. It was almost like having Jordan's parents there. Though he imagined Mr. Wood would've been able to pinpoint the minute Declan's feelings went from grateful client to *Could we be more?*

Mike threw a look Declan's way and his stomach tensed.

Declan cleared his throat. "She was helping me practice giving a guided tour for river fishing the first time."

"The first time?" Mike asked.

"I told you I was helping Declan," Jordan interjected. "Don't be so rude."

Mike threw his arms up in the air as if asking, *What?*

"Has anyone signed up for the fishing tour?" Vivian laid a hand on Mike. "What else are you offering, Declan?"

"They have. I'm also offering kayaking tours, hiking and team-building excursions."

"Don't forget camping," Jordan piped up. She met his gaze. "I think tourists will love it."

It meant a lot to him that she thought so. He resisted the urge to rub the back of his neck. "We'll see," Declan said. "I did get an inquiry for a team-building adventure for next Thursday and Friday, but I haven't responded yet."

Jordan's eyes lit up. "That's amazing. Are you going to take it?"

"No reason not to."

She smiled. "Good."

After that, conversation seemed to flow more easily, and Declan didn't feel as ridiculous as he had when he first sat down at the Woods' dining room table. When most folks had finished their plates of food, Declan offered to help clean up.

"I can help too if you'd like company," Jordan said.

"Yes, thanks." That would give him time to talk to her.

He took everyone's dishes to the kitchen. As he stacked them, Declan tried to think of a way to bridge the gap between them. Soon, he had the dining table cleared and walked toward the sink where Jordan stood rinsing off the dishes.

"It was kind of y'all to invite us for lunch." So not how he wanted to start, but whatever.

"Of course. The more, the merrier." Her smile seemed stiff.

Could she detect his nerves? If so, he better

get out what he wanted to say before the tension got the better of him.

"So, I've been thinking about something," he started.

"Yeah?"

He nodded, handing Jordan a dish to rinse off. "Um, if you'll give me a moment to talk so I can get this all out, then I'd like to hear your opinion."

"Of course, Declan. Go ahead."

Her stare burned a hole into his cheek, but he refused to meet her gaze. "I don't know about you, but I've been feeling these sparks between us." *Ugh.* He wanted to kick himself for using a word like that. But his befuddled mind couldn't think and attempt to wash the dishes at the same time.

"I didn't mean to say it like that."

Jordan stopped moving. "Then, what do you mean?"

"I, uh…" Declan turned to her and warmth filled his chest. A look of—tenderness?—filled Jordan's eyes. "I like you. But life is complicated, and I feel like I'm barely making it. Would you consider friendship?" He swallowed. "Because that's all I have to offer."

A light dimmed in her eyes. She went back to the dishes, turning on the water to rinse the one waiting in the sink. "Sure. That's fine."

Declan stuck out his hand, then winced. It was obvious Jordan didn't like what he'd had to say, and part of him wondered if that meant she liked him as well. So why had he made things worse by deciding to shake on it?

As her palm slid against his, a slight awareness made every nerve ending from his palm to his arm stand up. Considering this was supposed to be a friendly handshake, Declan would have to chalk up the sensation to relief that she had agreed, and not anything that would have him erasing the friendship lines he'd just drawn.

Chapter Fourteen

Jordan stared for the umpteenth time at the text Declan had sent this morning, wrestling on how to answer him.

Declan: Could you assist me in a team-building adventure? There will be ten people coming, and it's an overnight trip. Let me know as soon as you can.

The text had been sent an hour ago. Jordan couldn't possibly count the number of times she'd studied every word. Only knew plenty enough time had passed in order for her to reach for the antacids as she contemplated what to say.

Her heart still smarted from their talk on Sunday. Having Declan admit he liked her—oh happy day!—then ask for friendship had been like winning a giveaway only to find out she him—had activated some type of homing device inside her.

After placing the last product where it belonged, Jordan headed back for the checkout counter.

"Hey, Jordan?" Declan called out.

"Yes?"

"Do y'all have snack-size cheese?"

"Like string cheese?"

He shook his head. "Those ones that y'all had at lunch the other day. River would like some." His face reddened.

Was he embarrassed to bring up the fact that he was at her house because another customer had just entered the store, or maybe that he didn't know how to describe the cheese? Jordan navigated through the display racks and headed right for the section he'd overlooked.

"Here you go." She grabbed a pack and handed it to him. "That's the one River couldn't stop eating." The kid had stuffed his cheeks like a chipmunk.

Jordan had snapped a picture with her cell quickly before his cheeks deflated as he munched. She'd ended up texting the photo to Declan, laughing at how many emojis he'd used to convey his thanks.

"Thanks." His husky voice jarred her from memory lane.

Declan followed her to the counter, and she happily checked out all of his items. The faster he left, the quicker she could recalibrate her equilibrium, then bolster herself for the upcoming camping trip. Plus, she'd have to text Mike and let him know he'd need to cover for her in the store. The new homes he was building were almost finished, so working in the store shouldn't set him back too much.

"Tell River I said hi." Jordan pushed the brown paper bag toward Declan.

"Thanks. I will. See you Thursday."

She nodded and expelled a breath the moment the door closed behind him.

"Y'all are just the cutest couple," Mrs. Nance said as she placed her items on the counter. "I've always thought Declan Porter too nice of a man to remain single."

Jordan blinked back tears. "Uh, we're not a couple, Mrs. Nance. We just work together occasionally."

Her owlish eyes blinked behind red-framed eyeglasses. "Is that right?" She shook her head. "I know my eyesight is going, but I could have sworn I saw love in both of y'all's eyes." She shook her head again.

Jordan swallowed, trying to think of something else to say, but her brain had emptied in self-protection.

"You just never know nowadays. People not marrying as soon as they used to. Playing hard to get." She huffed. "I don't know how your generation manages to find that someone special."

"Me either." At least that Jordan could agree on.

The whole Traun fiasco still had Jordan shaking her head. Yet she had to admit that it had done her a favor in sending her back to Willow Springs, where she needed to be. She'd been talking to God more, hanging around her brothers more and even reaching out to Pippen more than when she'd resided in Fayetteville. How sad that it took moving back home for her to reach out to her sibling who had lived just a few miles away from her. Then again, neither were battling back grief as intensely as before.

The time back in Willow Springs had revealed that her hometown held her heart, and she wanted to make her mark here.

She could only pray that these feelings for Declan would diminish so she could find someone who was willing to take a chance on her. *Lord, please don't let the camping trip obliterate my heart. I need divine shields up to remember that Declan only wants friendship.* She recalled the look of astonishment on his face when she'd admitted that she liked him.

Yeah, Thursday's excursion would be interesting.

* * *

She *liked* him.

The words had echoed in Declan's head for the past two days. Along with the picture of Jordan squeezing her eyes shut as she confessed her feelings. What she'd left out was how much she liked him. He understood the basics, she wanted to be more than friends, but what Declan couldn't figure out was if her feelings felt anything like his.

But did it matter? He purposely chose friendship because of his past baggage—knowing how messed up his life had become after his divorce. How could he trust Jordan not to do the same thing further down the line? If he took a chance, asked her out, then fell for her, what would he do if she left Willow Springs and never returned? He'd had enough of abandonment.

Yet half of him wanted to take back his offer of friendship after Jordan had confessed her feelings. The idea of having another person around to do life with was appealing—all the more so when that person was Jordan. Yet the other half knew that his life really was a mess.

Brendan had recently informed him that Mekayla had been furious over the child support request. Since Declan had blocked her number—at Brendan's counsel—and made Brendan the point of contact, he'd dodged that conversation. However, Brendan had retold the story with enough details that Declan could imagine his ex-wife's ire.

Brendan was sure that a judge would agree to child support and that Declan wouldn't have to pay the loan amount she requested, considering they were married when she gave Declan the money. It also helped their case that she hadn't contributed in any way to River's upbringing the past four years.

Once this camping trip was over with, Declan would finally be able to put some money into his business's savings account. Something he'd never been able to do but had always wanted to. For all intents and purposes, Declan's life was looking up.

Still, there was always that proverbial shoe ready to drop and ruin any hope he had in the future. Not to mention the question that had plagued Declan since Jordan's declaration of interest. Was he denying River a chance to have a happy childhood with two parents—even if one would be considered a stepmom? There was no doubt in Declan's mind that Jordan cared for River. But that also meant if she left, River stood the chance of being rejected by two mothers.

Declan dragged a hand down his face and closed the trailer. He'd loaded everything they'd need for the next two days. Now was the time to get his head in the game, not to wonder about Jordan. He'd just have to make sure any thoughts related to his personal life stayed buried while on this tour.

His stomach heaved knowing that Jordan acting as another tour guide could potentially solidify their friendship-only status. As much as he believed there were little sparks between them, he hadn't expected her to admit she felt the same way.

Had she as much trouble as Declan keeping their relationship labeled under business? After all, she was his consultant, observing and instructing him on ways to better run Porter Adventures. In the beginning, Declan had believed Jordan simply put up with him. As more and more looks were exchanged between them, he'd hoped she was attracted to him, as much as he hoped neither one of them would act on it. Once they did, he'd have to worry about potential heartache.

At least agreeing to friendship spared them a potential breakup. Only Declan couldn't tell left from right now.

Lord God, what am I going to do? How do I reconcile my plans with an alternate future? Was there somewhere in the Bible that gave advice on that?

A man's heart deviseth his way: but the Lord directeth his steps.

Declan winced. Was that what he was doing? Planning his own way and leaving no room for the Lord to direct his steps? Declan blew out a breath.

I'm sorry, Lord. Please direct me. Please tell me what to do.

Declan started the engine, then put the gear to Drive. He was going to pick up Jordan, then head toward the campsite where ten employees from Ballanger Advertisement would meet them. Tonight they would camp out, and tomorrow they would be staying at Simplicity Rentals before returning to Bentonville.

The part of the plan that had Declan's stomach churning was the car ride from the general store to the campsite, alone…with Jordan. Would it be strained? Would Declan confess and share his own conflicting feelings?

He alternated between praying for guidance and worrying over what would happen until he pulled into the general store's parking lot. Jordan sat in a rocking chair and stood when the car came to a stop. She grabbed a duffel bag off the front porch and headed his way.

Declan stepped out and rounded the front of the car. "I can take that for you."

She raised her eyebrows. "Is there no room in the back seats?"

"There is."

"Then I've got it."

His neck heated. Mistake number one. "Right. Okay." He headed back for the driver's seat. Maybe he should have done more praying over the trip than ruminating over his tenuous relationship with Jordan.

As he drove away from the general store, Declan's mind thought of talking point after talking point. But he shot them all down. None of them seemed right. Wasn't being friends supposed to get rid of the awful small talk between folks who didn't know each other?

"Are we going to talk or just sit in silence the whole way?" Jordan asked.

He glanced at her, then back at the road. "I was trying to think of what to say."

"How about what funny things River has said lately? Or what you expect from me as your second guide? Or what I should know about the team that's meeting us at the campground? You know, the normal stuff."

Declan huffed out a laugh, running a hand through his hair. "Yeah. I can answer all of those."

"Good. Then maybe we won't have to sit here sweating bullets. Aren't we friends?"

He spared her another glance. "We are."

She lifted the corners of her mouth in a genuine smile. "Then relax, Declan. Everything will be fine."

He heard her, he really did. But Declan couldn't help but think how badly he'd messed up their relationship by friend-zoning one of the most amazing women he'd ever known. Still, he wanted her to know how much he appreciated the effort she'd put forth by continuing his fiasco of a suggestion.

"Thanks, Jordan."

"Sure. Now get to talking, boss man. I need to know everything."

He explained the ins and outs of the trip. His plan for the company to grow closer as a group. Some of the tasks he'd found online and others he incorporated—activities that were easier for two to do. Pairing up the guests would allow for one-on-one interactions and for Declan to switch the pairs with the different activities.

"That sounds great. They're going to love it," Jordan said.

"You think?"

"Yes. You've got this. Don't doubt. You know God will cover you."

He did. Declan had planned this trip, but he was trusting God to direct his steps. Funny how he had no problem doing that in business, but trusting God in his personal life made him want to break out in hives.

"Do you mind if I pray for us?" Jordan asked.

His eyebrows rose in surprise. "Really?"

"Yeah. I've been exercising my prayer muscles lately."

He chuckled. "Always a good thing to do. Please."

"Heavenly Father, thank You for giving us the opportunity to lead a group into team-building exercises. We pray if there is any strife, that this trip will bring healing. We pray if there is miscommunication, that understanding will come. We pray that we bring You glory as we lead these men and women. We pray they have fun and that this will only be the beginning for Porter Adventures."

Declan swallowed, agreeing with Jordan. But he was also getting a picture of what could be their future—going out into nature together for the glory of God. The very idea raised the hairs on his arms and seemed to remove blinders from his eyes.

"Thank You for watching over us. In Jesus's name we pray. Amen." Jordan whispered the last part, as if caught up in the reverence of praying to the Creator.

"Amen," he echoed, overcome.

Jordan squeezed his arm, then promptly let

go. "We're going to have a blast, just you wait and see."

"I believe you."

After that prayer, how could this be anything but a success? Maybe not in all the ways men of the world counted success, but if Declan left tomorrow evening knowing he'd done his best, that relationships were strengthened among the employees, then he'd done what God had asked of him, what Jordan believed he could do. And that would be success enough for him.

Now if he could figure out the prayer that would guide him in his relationship with Jordan...

Chapter Fifteen

Declan was so adorably nervous.

As they drew closer to the campground, he grew more fidgety, tapping a mindless rhythm on the steering wheel while muttering under his breath. Jordan was pretty sure those mutters were actual prayers, so she kept quiet, adding her own petitions to God on Declan's behalf. Even if they weren't praying together, surely their individual pleas would echo one another's in ways unseen.

Thank goodness they served an all-knowing God. Since Jordan had returned to Willow Springs, her faith had grown. She went from believing that God ignored her, was maybe even upset with her, to realizing it was Jordan's own insecurities that had altered her view of God. He was still a good God, a good Father, a good provider. Just because Traun had failed Jordan didn't mean that God ever would. And just because she'd believed her family expected less of her didn't mean God had. He knew her capabilities because He fashioned them.

Those small revelations had released invisible chains from Jordan. She could now pray with more ease, not expecting to fail God but enjoying a conversation with Him. She also realized that God, at the basic level, wanted Jordan to love Him and love others. Somehow she'd been expecting her purpose to be more detailed and accompanied by a light-bulb moment that would clue her in. Only, her understanding had been gradual in the quiet moments of prayer and reflection.

Jordan had been created for a relationship with God and for a relationship with the people He'd placed in her life. People like her siblings, Vivian and those she knew from church. And of course, Declan and River. Jordan loved them all, and for different reasons. Still, loving them as God directed was part of her purpose on this earth.

After spending time with her Bible last night, she'd come to a conclusion. Declan didn't have to love her back.

Wait? Love?

Her breath hitched. Jordan hadn't thought of that word once when exploring the feelings she had for Declan Porter. She laid a hand on her racing heart. Could she seriously be in love? Sure, Jordan already knew she liked Declan, but that was an entirely different playing field than love. Love meant…her mind thought of the first book of Corinthians.

No person could grow up in church without learning about chapter 13 and how it described love. Did she have it in her to love Declan wholly, even if he didn't love her back? He'd only asked her to be his friend.

Lord God, if that's what Declan needs, that's what I'll do. She understood how a complicated life could leave you on uneven footing and how friends were like a life preserver in the midst of those storms. Jordan needed to operate like there was no guarantee that Declan would ever return her feelings.

But there's also no guarantee he won't.

Still, she wouldn't enter a friendship with him expecting it to turn into more. She could be there for him as a friend because she had the power *and* the strength of God's grace to be his friend. Being *just friends* would allow her to be around River, maybe even be some kind of maternal figure to him. Not that she could ever take a mother's place, but Jordan wanted him to know he was loved. If she could do her part to ensure that River never felt abandoned or question God's love for him, she would.

She sniffed just as Declan stopped the car. "We're here."

"Oh, good." Her voice came out a croak. Jordan winced inwardly.

"You okay?"

"Frog in my throat," she mumbled, stepping down from the car. She reached for her duffel bag in the back, knowing her water bottle was in it. After taking a swig, she slid her arms through the straps so she could wear the bag like a backpack.

Declan blinked at her. "That's pretty ingenious."

She grinned. "I thought so."

"You never cease to surprise me, Jordan Wood."

"What do you mean?" She tilted her head.

Declan propped his foot on the back of the trailer, resting his elbow on his thigh. "I thought for sure you would *not* be into nature when I came to ask y'all for help selling all the items I requested."

"We live in Willow Springs. How can I not love nature?" She placed her hands on her hips, an amused grin on her face.

"You know Cecelia?"

She nodded.

"She can't stand nature. She cried during our senior picnic."

Jordan recalled the memory vividly. "I thought she'd been dumped."

Declan chuckled. "Dumped into the great outdoors."

"You were waiting for that, weren't you?"

"'Bout time I can prove my brain operates faster than a sloth. I can be witty." He winked.

Her heart wanted to swoon, but she gave herself a mental smack with a reminder that they were just friends. "Sure you can." She cleared her throat, searching for firm footing. A charming Declan was a dangerous Declan. "That's why it took you a month to have a quick comeback ready."

He laughed, ignoring her teasing.

Jordan breathed out a sigh. This was going to work. She was going to be Declan's friend, even if she experienced a pang of longing every now and again.

A black van pulled into the lot.

"Think that's them?" she asked.

"Probably."

People began filing out of the vehicle once it parked, and Jordan counted them silently. "Ten," she said for Declan's benefit.

"Yeah, I recognize one guy. He sent a copy of his license with payment."

"Good." She clapped her hands together. "Then let's get this show on the road."

A forced grin covered Declan's face.

Jordan stepped closer. "Remember from our prayers—God's got this. *You've* got this. You won't fail."

He blew out a breath. "Thanks, Jordan." He pulled her to his chest, wrapping his arms around her.

She hugged him back, cataloging the woodsy scent that was distinctly Declan. She never wanted to leave the comfort of his embrace but withdrew to maintain the boundaries he'd set. "Put on that Porter Adventure persona and let's rock this."

His grin was much surer this time. Jordan followed a few steps behind Declan as he went to greet the owner of the company. She eyed the rest of the people. Some looked nervous, some disinterested, and others were excited. It would be quite the mix, but one Jordan knew Declan could handle. She said another prayer for him, then stepped up to be introduced. No matter what happened, she'd count this trip a success even if she had to figure out something basic to cheer Declan up with afterward.

Jordan had been right. So far, the team-building excursion was going great. There had been some hesitancy from a few of the men and women. Some obviously had never stepped foot in nature other than walking to and from their car, while others were clearly enthusiasts and great encouragers. Declan would engage them when the feeling that he was floundering came his way. Sometimes, he'd find Jordan's gaze. She always had a ready thumbs-up or a simple smile to keep him from panicking.

After a day of hiking, they came to the campsite Declan had reserved. The hike had been fun, with a few stops here and there to throw in some team-building exercises, but he was glad the end of the day was in sight. The last hour, the team had started to grumble as they entered the hangry zone.

Declan called Jordan to him.

"What's up?" she asked quietly.

"We need to get tents set up and food prepped so we can eat."

She nodded, studying him. "Do you have an idea of who you want to do what?"

Declan explained the groups he'd mentally put together based off today's activities. "What do you think?" He watched her face for any hesitancy, though he knew she'd be honest if his idea didn't hold merit.

"I'd switch Parker with Jon."

Declan tilted his head to peer at the two. After watching them a few seconds, he agreed. "Good idea. Do you want to lead the tent crew or food crew?"

"Food crew."

He grinned. "Great. I wanted tent crew anyway."

She chuckled, lightly pushing on his arm. "Then get the tents ready, slacker."

"Yes, chef."

The sound of Jordan's laughter went with him as he yelled out to the five people on the tent crew. He explained their chore and that it would be two to one tent. He scanned the area, telling them where he wanted the canvases to be set up since there would be seven total. He and Jordan would each be in a separate one while the employees would all have a buddy in their overnight accommodations.

Time passed as everyone set out to their tasks. By the time they had all the tents erected, Jordan called out, informing everyone dinner had been prepared. She placed a bottle of sanitizer on the end of a foldout table and a package of towelettes next to it.

Declan glanced at his hands, realizing he'd need both sanitizer and a towelette to get some of this dirt off.

Soon he settled on a log, enjoying a burger and some potato chips. Jordan took the space next to him, her plate filled with a couple of beef hot dogs and fruit.

"No chips?" he asked.

Her nose wrinkled. "I don't like the crunchy noise in my ear."

He just stared at her slack-jawed, and she laughed, then shrugged. "What can I say? I may talk loud, but I don't need to hear so much noise in my head."

"That has to be the most interesting reason I've ever heard someone give for not eating chips."

"I'm strange."

Nah, she was about perfect. He blinked down at his food, trying to shake the thought loose. Had he chosen the right path? Just because Jordan liked nature, could gut a fish like a pro and hike without complaint didn't mean she was perfect for him. Neither did the way her face lit up for River and the amusement she showed when he talked endlessly about dinosaurs. That just meant she made a good friend.

"How do you feel about the day?" Jordan asked quietly.

Declan met her gaze then stared out into the group. "I think we've done well."

She bumped his shoulder. "*You've* done well. I'm just backup."

"I appreciate you helping."

"My pleasure." She took a bite of her food.

He listened as nature serenaded them. "How do you think everyone will do tomorrow?"

"I think they'll love it. Who doesn't want to go down a river on a kayak?"

"Melissa?" His chin lifted toward the woman in question.

Jordan cracked a smile. "I bet she'll come around. She just doesn't like bugs."

"Yeah, well, welcome to the Natural State."

"Everything will turn out just fine tomorrow. You'll see, Declan Porter."

He chuckled. "Why are you calling me by my full name?"

"Is it though?" She tilted her head. "Something tells me you have a spectacular middle name that would work well in a scolding. Did your grandma ever break out the three names?"

Declan had to laugh, because his grandma had used them often. "Maybe."

"Hmm. What about you? Have you done that to River?"

He shook his head. "He doesn't have a middle name."

"Why not?"

"Mekayla thought it archaic."

Jordan's bottom lip poked out.

"What?"

244 Winning His Trust

"Nothing. I have nothing nice to say." She took a bite of food.

"Been there. You'll overcome those feelings."

She turned to him. "Have you? Are all of your feelings toward Mekayla resolved?"

"Funny you asked. I was asking God the same thing the other day, especially considering this latest fiasco."

"What did He say? Or what conclusion did you come to?" Jordan asked softly.

"That I can't control her. I thought about it—even went so far as to try to see if I could make her use her visitation rights. But that was a dead end. So I'll take care of my son and remember how much of a blessing that is. She could have left me and taken River with her. But she trusted him with me. I need to look at it from a glass-half-full perspective."

"Wow. That's pretty amazing."

Declan nodded. "Agreed. What's even more amazing is I'm finally going to ask for child support."

Her eyes widened. "Wait, you haven't been receiving any financial help?" She set her empty plate on the ground in front of her.

"No."

Jordan's mouth dropped open, then closed, then opened once more. Why wouldn't he?

"Wow. Now I know the trick to making you speechless." He smirked.

"Oh, Declan." She shook her head. "I think I earned the right to know that middle name now, sir. You definitely need a scolding."

"Spare me. Brendan already got me. But…" He sighed, staring into her pretty face. "It's Ames. Declan Ames Porter."

Jordan grinned. "Love it."

"What about you? Do you have a middle name, or would that mess up the dream team effect?"

She groaned, dropping her head into her hands. "Please don't ask."

"Oh, this I have to hear." He rubbed his hands. "Should I guess?"

"No." Her head popped up and she narrowed her eyes. "Besides, you'll never guess correctly."

"This sounds like a challenge."

"It's not." She huffed, but her lips twitched.

"If I guess correctly—"

"You do *not* get my firstborn."

Declan's head fell back as his laughter filled the air. When he was done laughing, he noticed some of the employees staring at him like he had two heads. He shrugged, hoping to convey, *What can I say, sorry?* in his expression. Then he turned to Jordan. "I won't take your firstborn. Promise."

"You say it so solemnly, but I can see the laughter in your eyes, Declan Ames Porter."

"Hey, if you're throwing around three names, then I want the same honor."

"Guess. Three guesses." She held up the same number of fingers.

"Ann."

She rolled her eyes. "No." She dropped a finger.

Okay, he had to pull out the big guns. He had no idea what names were popular twenty-eight years ago and would fit a basketball theme. Had Declan ever heard Big Mike's, Chuck's or Pippen's middle name? Of course not. They hadn't been that close in school.

"You give up already?" Jordan taunted.

"No, no. Just reviewing my options."

"You know there are millions of names, right?"

"Then that means I have a chance."

She chuckled, settling her hand on her chin. "Then I guess I'll wait. Hopefully you'll decide before it's time to turn in. I'll need my beauty rest for tomorrow's activities."

Declan glanced around. A few of the others were yawning. It would probably be best to mandate a lights-out for everyone *after* they've cleaned up. "Fine. Mary?"

"Nope, it's not religious."

"Do you have any other hints?"

"Nope." She smacked her lips. "I don't want you to guess it. I like it when I can say Declan Ames Porter versus you being able to use my whole name."

"Why don't I just look at your driver's license?"

"You'll have to find it first." She wagged a finger. "One guess left. What's it going to be?"

His mind filtered through names, trying to match one to the other. Finally, he threw his hands up. "I don't know. Michael?"

Jordan's mouth dropped open.

"Wait?" He straightened. "I got it right? It's Michael?"

She narrowed her gaze. "How's it spelled?"

His breath came in spurts. If she asked that question, that meant it wasn't spelled like the masculine version. "Uh… M?"

She arched a brow.

"I."

She made a motion with her hand to keep going.

"K?" He winced inwardly, waiting for her to disagree.

But when her jaw dropped once more, Declan fist-pumped.

"No cheering yet, buddy. You still have more letters to go."

"But do I really need to continue? You said to guess your middle name, not how it's spelled."

"Spelling matters." Jordan crossed her arms in a pout.

She was beautiful and made him want to laugh as well. "Okay. A-E-L?"

Her shoulders dropped. "How in the world did you ever guess that right?"

"God must have been on my side." He bumped her gently, wanting to wrap an arm around her instead.

"Guess we'll both be using full names when the need calls for it."

"Guess so." He smiled. "Ready to clean up?"

She groaned. "Yes. Let's get this over with."

Declan laughed, then called the group together. This time, he switched the chores. Tent crew now had food clean up, and food crew would ensure the equipment was ready to go for tomorrow.

By the time Declan crawled into his tent a little while later and settled in to say his prayers, all he could do was thank God for Jordan's company.

Chapter Sixteen

Every muscle in her body ached. Jordan huffed as she crawled out of her tent and tried to stretch her back. Yet arching it only made it feel tighter and reaching for her toes didn't feel much better. Had she been smart and packed some pain reliever? Thinking of today's activities made her want to crawl right back into her sleeping bag and wake up tomorrow when it was all over.

Only she'd feel awful if she left Declan with the crowd. She scanned the area to see if he'd awoken yet. Her eyes widened as she spied everyone getting ready and putting away the tents. Jordan scrambled toward Declan. How long had she slept?

A quick glance at her watch showed it was seven.

"Did I oversleep?" she asked, once close to Declan.

His face brightened. "Good morning. And no. I woke up an hour ago, and one by one, they all just started popping out of their tents. Some of them wanted to get a head start. So no worries, you didn't snooze too late."

She blew out a breath. "Still, I'm sorry I didn't wake up sooner."

"I handled everything. Plus got a crew to start breakfast, which is almost done." He pointed to the people manning the fire.

"Great. Please tell me there's some instant coffee or something."

Declan laughed. "Not a morning person?"

"I am when I'm expecting it. Seems like it snuck up on me. I still need a few more hours."

"Ain't that the truth." A bemused expression covered his face. "River hates the morning."

"So does Mike."

An interesting gleam entered Declan's blue eyes. Jordan brushed away the urge to lean closer. That was something friends did *not* do.

"Does Michael have your first name for a middle name?"

Jordan's lips curved. "I'll never tell."

Declan laughed, and Jordan felt like she'd just won a prize.

"That's answer enough."

"You heard nothing from me."

Jordan walked away, needing a cup of coffee stat to wake her brain and remind herself of the plan. Friends, and that was it. None of this extra smiling, exuberant laughing or sneaking glances Declan's way. She just needed to rein herself in, since sleeping had seemed to dislodge a few loose screws.

She grabbed a tin cup, then poured liquid gold into it before searching for the creamer. Soon, she had a biscuit and sausage patty ready to fill up her stomach before they completed Declan's agenda for the day. She'd meant to review today's activities before going to sleep last night but had crashed almost as soon as her head hit the pillow.

Then Jordan had woken up in the middle of the night, realizing she'd missed her nightly prayers. A quick thank-you for how the day had turned out, coupled with prayers for continued safety and fun, allowed her to fall right back to sleep.

She eyed the space her tent occupied, one of the few still up. She needed to get her items packed away before she had to climb into a kayak. Was she going to be paired up with someone?

The employees from Ballanger happily chatted as they ate and drank the morning's provisions. Jordan tried to figure out who Declan would pair together so she'd have no surprises.

Plus, he'd probably ask for her opinion on the grouping.

Since yesterday, part of Jordan had been thinking how wonderful it would be to do this full time. Porter Adventures was a far cry from the boutique she'd worked at in Fayetteville, but being out in nature helped her breathe easier. It was like she could relax and stop carrying the weight of the stress she'd been lugging before. Maybe she could work for Declan part time if Michael ever hired another person to work in the general store. Didn't Willow Springs have any teenagers who needed a job?

Worry about that when you return home. For now, she needed to find out what Declan wanted her help with.

After they got everything stowed away, they set out on a hike. The bright blue skies and perfect temps made the morning journey toward the river pleasant. They also had an added bonus of singing. One of the employees—Kris?—sang in her church choir back home. She led them in a song that filled Jordan's spirit and made her beam into the heaven's cloudless skies. The Lord had made the perfect day with the perfect weather. The only thing that would make it better was if Declan decided he didn't want to remain just friends but wanted to take a chance on a dating relationship.

She blew out a breath. *Sorry Lord. I told myself I wouldn't do this, that I'd just be happy with the boundaries he set. I have to respect them.* Especially if she wanted to continue to have a welcome presence in Declan's life.

When they reached their destination, they set out to place the kayaks that had been waiting for them along the riverbanks, Declan went over the safety rules. Jordan inspected everyone's life jackets for proper wear as he continued to talk. Before they'd even started on their hike, Declan had explained who would be paired up. His thought was the more experienced kayakers needed to go with one less experienced.

Once Jordan had finished the safety check, she stopped next to the kayak she'd be going in. Declan had assigned Morgan to her. The guy had never been in a kayak but said he was a good swimmer. Jordan hoped he was paying attention to Declan's presentation. Her eyes scanned the faces for his and breathed out a sigh of relief when she saw him gazing intently at Declan.

Lord, please keep us all safe.

She almost rolled her eyes at herself. They were all in life jackets. What could possibly go wrong?

Declan broke up the group, and everyone started for the riverbank.

Jordan smiled at Morgan as he drew closer. "Ready?"

He nodded. "It seemed simple enough."

"Good. I love kayaking. Once you get the hang of it, you'll wonder why you haven't done it before."

Morgan chuckled. "I hope so. I'm a little nervous."

"Do you want to ride in the front or the back?" She'd actually prefer the front, but maybe the front would make him feel safer.

"Uh, the front please."

Bummer. But she put an easy smile on her face. "Sure. You can get in first." Jordan moved to the back, waiting for Morgan to get settled before she took the spot behind him.

Declan gave the okay for everyone to take to the river. Jordan's kayak would go first, with Declan's taking the end of their trail. She exhaled, enjoying the breeze on her face and the heat from the sun. The kayak wobbled and Jordan looked forward.

"Be sure to alternate strokes on each side of the kayak," Jordan advised Morgan. He was beginning to make them turn toward the left.

He nodded and swooped the paddle on the left side so hard the boat tilted.

"Whoa, not so hard!" Jordan called.

But it was too late. His next stroke overturned

their kayak. Jordan tried to hold her breath before being submerged, but the sudden movement had her inhaling water unexpectedly. Her body flew backward, and a sharp pain jabbed the back of her head. She tried to propel upward and not swallow more water, but something had her stuck. Her movements jerked as she tried to free herself, but the motion made her head spin, and pain rolled through her.

Help me, Lord!

Then the world faded to black.

The blood drained right out of Declan's face as Jordan's body submerged. Instinct took over as he rapidly paddled toward the front. Morgan's head popped up, and immediately the man started swimming to the shore. But Jordan hadn't broken the water's surface.

How was that possible? Was she stuck? Was she hurt? *God, please let me get there in time.*

Gauging the distance, Declan flung off his life vest and jumped into the water. His heart surged in his chest as he spotted Jordan's body. Her vest had hooked onto a rocky riverbank. He freed her vest, and immediately her body went upward.

Declan broke free, dragging in a lungful of air. He hooked an arm around Jordan as he trudged toward the shore. He placed her on her back, tilted up her chin and breathed into her mouth once…twice. "Wake up, baby, please," he murmured.

Then he began chest compressions.

"I called 911," a voice shouted.

Declan nodded, still counting the compressions. *Eight, nine, ten.* Jordan's body jerked, and he immediately rolled her onto the side as water dribbled out of her mouth. He eased her head onto his lap to keep her neck from angling downward.

"How far out is the ambulance?" Declan called out.

"Twenty minutes."

"I'm so sorry, I'm so sorry," Morgan mumbled, standing next to Declan.

"Jordan, can you hear me?" he murmured in her ear. But she lay there moaning, eyes still closed.

Declan couldn't think. Since Jordan was having a medical emergency, he couldn't focus on the Ballanger group. But could he just leave them out in the middle of the forest while he took care of Jordan?

God, a little guidance, please.

He swallowed as the panic threatened to overwhelm him. Drawing out his cell phone from its waterproof case, he selected one of the favorites in his contact list and pressed call.

"Willow Springs Medical Clinic, this is Charles Wood, how may I help you?"

"Chuck. Jordan's hurt. She went underwater. We called 911, but we're at—" He looked at the map, then rattled off the coordinates. "What do I do?"

"Breathe, man."

Right. Declan could do that. Hadn't he created a plan for being in just this type of situation? *Yeah, but that was before the possibly injured party was the love of my life.* He blinked, staring at Jordan's still body.

Oh no. Why would he realize how much he cared about her now, when she was hurt and there was nothing for him to do about it? He couldn't call her and take her out to an amazing restaurant, or even just go stargazing while looking into her beautiful dark brown eyes and telling her she was the light of his life.

No, he was trying to get her help before there was nothing to share but heartache from regrets.

"Do you know if she hit her head or anything?" Chuck asked.

"Let me check." Carefully, Declan checked her damp hair, which had curled, for a lump. He stopped when something sticky touched his fingertips. Withdrawing a hand, he grimaced at the blood on his fingers.

"Yes. It's bleeding."

"If someone still has 911 on the line, tell them you need an airlift. She'll need to be checked for bleeding."

Declan frowned, eyes roaming over Jordan's frame. "I just told you she was."

"I'm talking about internally. They'll need to check for a brain bleed, Declan."

His mouth dried. "Oh no."

Kris thrust a phone into his face. "They're asking for coordinates."

Declan took the cell, relaying the information and listening to the emergency operator's instructions. He relayed Chuck's advice on an airlift as well.

After ending the call with 911, Declan relayed the plan to Chuck and slid his phone back into his pocket. Declan talked to the Ballanger group supervisor, who informed him that one of their guys was confident he could get them back to the campsite, then to their van. Declan passed his map with the route to the guys, with a reminder to call if they needed help and to text when they made it to the parking lot without issue.

Morgan apologized one too many times during the process, and finally, they dragged him away.

A few minutes later, he heard the whir of a chopper and watched as the EMTs slid a neck brace on Jordan, transferred her onto a harness, then headed back toward the helicopter. Declan had been given permission to ride along.

As the aircraft rose into the air, Declan bowed his head and prayed.

Lord God, I beg for Your protection for Jordan right now. Please bring healing to her body with no complications. I ask that You keep the first responders safe and that we make it to the hospital in one piece. Please comfort Jordan's family and even myself.

Declan drew in a breath, his eyelids beginning to feel hot. *And I pray, Lord, that I'll get the opportunity to let Jordan know how I feel. That I won't be a coward, because if this is how my heart feels thinking I've lost a chance with her forever, I'll gladly risk it for a chance to just date her.*

Still, Declan wanted to believe that this wasn't the end of their story. He wanted to believe that somehow, some way, God would give him the opportunity to be with Jordan and have a long-lasting future with her. To create the family River desperately wanted and that Declan had been too afraid to admit he craved.

Please, Lord.

When they arrived at the hospital, the staff directed him to the waiting area, where he could remain out of their way. When the doors closed in front of him, Jordan hidden behind them, his heart dropped to his toes.

Please let her be okay. Please.

The longer he waited, the more he prayed. When her family showed up, he gave them updates, then took up vigil once more with whispered pleas. He wouldn't stop praying until the doctors informed him she was alive and well.

Chapter Seventeen

Jordan walked down the stairs and into the general store. She couldn't stay in her bed or on the couch any longer. She was slowly dying of boredom, had been since she'd awoken in the hospital and learned of the concussion she'd been diagnosed with.

Thankfully, there was no lasting damage from being underwater and taking a drink of the Buffalo River.

She'd received a gift card to her favorite online retailer from the Ballanger group, specifically Morgan. They all wished her well and had already booked a repeat tour with Declan. Relief had flooded her at knowing she hadn't lost Declan much-needed business.

The downside of having a concussion was the lack of TV and other electronics. She received the occasional text from Declan, but he'd been strangely absent from her life. Did he feel guilty? The one man she wanted to see more of in her life—her brothers were around too much—and he hadn't bothered to check on her. She told herself not to be upset, but she missed Declan Ames Porter.

Her brothers seemed to be taking up slack from Declan's absence. Mike had catered to her every whim. Turned up the thermostat when she'd been too cold and turned it down when she'd been too warm. He even made her her favorite foods and played board games with her when she was up for it. Chuck had stopped by every evening after work to make sure she was okay and join them in the fun. Only as the week had progressed and her feelings spiraled from being ignored by Declan, her brothers had chosen to stay away.

Jordan wasn't trying to be difficult, but not seeing the Porter men had soured her disposition. The boredom didn't help any either.

"What are you doing down here?" Mike asked, lines furrowing his brow.

Goodness, he had more wrinkles than a Shar-Pei. Jordan blew out a breath. "I need something to do."

"You have something to do. It's called healing." He pointed toward the staircase. "Now go back upstairs and let your body do that work."

"Mike..." Jordan whined.

He squeezed the bridge of his nose. "I'm going to make you go hang out with Chuck."

Her eyes widened. "Do you think he'll put me to work?" She wouldn't mind going to the clinic. Maybe she could answer phone calls or file paperwork or handle whatever nonmedical grunt work they needed done.

"No. I'm actually praying he'll put you in one of their rooms and sign you in as a patient."

She pursed her lips. "So funny."

"What's funny—" Mike crossed his arms and leaned against the counter "—is you thinking you can just jump back into work after surviving a concussion that bad."

"I didn't die." Though from what the doctors and Chuck had relayed, it had been a very serious injury.

"Thank the good Lord, but I might die from your stubbornness," Mike groused.

Jordan grinned and walked over to her big brother and hugged him. "You're the best. I love you."

"I haven't done anything for such high praise."

"I heard positive affirmations take away the grouchiness."

Mike huffed, then returned her hug. "You made me this way."

"Sure." Jordan pulled away and smirked at

him. "I think you made me like this first, so it's up to you to fix the whole situation."

He peered down at her. "How does your head feel?"

Like she needed to take a pain reliever. Instead she said, "Better than yesterday." Which was true. She just wasn't healing as fast as she'd like.

"Really?"

Yes, because now she didn't want to either puke or still her stomach every time she moved. "Really. But I desperately need to get out of the house."

Mike sighed. "What if you go back and rest, and I send some friends over to keep you company?"

Unless it was Declan, she didn't want to make small talk with anyone. Why was he avoiding her?

Part of her was surprised, because she thought she remembered him calling her *baby*. Then again that most likely had been her concussed brain messing with her dreams and having her believe they had been reality. Since a whole week had passed without any indication from Declan that they were more than friends, she had to believe it had all been a figment of her imagination.

"What friends?" Jordan asked softly.

"Well, Eryn called to talk. When I told her what happened, I had to plead with her not to visit."

Jordan bit her lip. "I saw the flowers she sent." Her stomach still twisted whenever she thought of her ex-roommates. Maxine still hadn't reached out to Jordan.

"Did you thank her?" His brows rose in anticipation of her answer.

She nodded. "We texted back and forth briefly. I went out on a limb and told her we could get together once I was feeling better." She blew out a breath. "But I'm not ready for her visit right now." Maybe she should just go back upstairs. "I think I'll go lie down."

The mention of *friend* made her want to cry as she thought of Declan once again.

A relieved expression filled her brother's face. "Good. Go back upstairs. I'll call Vivian when you're ready for company."

"Thanks, Mike."

"Of course. Do you want me to ask Chuck to come over for dinner tonight?"

Jordan grinned. "Yes, please. Make him bring something from the Sassy Spoon," she suggested.

"What do you want from there?"

Jordan froze, thinking about what sounded good. "Pot pie?"

"Chicken?"

Was there any other kind? "Yes, please."

"You got it."

Jordan climbed the stairs back up to the home floor, then walked right back into the living room, where she'd been stationed most of the week. She was so tempted to scream in frustration, but that surely wouldn't help her recover from the concussion any sooner. Neither would watching a show—there *had* to be something bingeable just waiting for her—or playing a mindless game on her phone. Being inactive was the one thing she hated most.

Why Lord? Why did I have to get injured? How will You use that for good?

Or maybe it wouldn't be used for good. Maybe it was just something that had happened, and no ripple effect would come about.

A knock sounded on the door and Jordan frowned. Chuck had started walking in without knocking. He wouldn't pick now to knock, would he? Then again, Mike had said he'd ask him over for dinner, not lunch. Though from the rumblings going on in her middle, she could use a midday meal. Why hadn't she asked for that instead of talking about dinner?

She crossed the room and twisted the handle. She blinked at the visitor standing on the landing.

"Declan." Her heart bounced in her chest, happiness filling her with warmth at his presence.

"Hey, Jordan. May I come in?"

"Oh, right." She shook her head, then muffled a groan at the movement. She stepped back, waving a hand for him to come in. That was much safer.

"How you feeling?"

"I could use a pain reliever." Hadn't she meant to grab some after talking to Mike?

"Where is it?" Declan looked around the room.

Jordan pointed to the pill bottle on the countertop, and Declan headed for it.

"Do you need water?" he asked.

"No, thank you. I have some over here." She sat down, mentally trying to prepare for Declan's visit. Why was he here now?

But as much as the question danced around her head, the happiness from simply seeing him didn't abate. She took in his hair, which looked a bit long at the ears. His eyes were a little shadowed, but other than that, he looked good—*really* good.

"Oh, I brought food." He pointed to the brown paper bag he'd set down. "Nothing fancy, but I thought you'd like something since it's near lunchtime."

"You're a wonderful friend."

His lips flattened, a tick in his jaw appearing.

Had she said something wrong? She waited for him to speak, but it was like he had to gather his thoughts.

Then a forced smile covered his mouth, and he stuck out a hand, a couple of pills laying in his palm. "Who knew all I had to do was feed you to get sweet talk?"

"Ha! River figured it out pretty quickly. He's always supplying me with his fish crackers."

Declan chuckled. "Better than him sharing his sandwich with you."

"So what did you bring?" She pointed to the bag he seemed to have forgotten. It wasn't from the Sassy Spoon.

"Oh. I actually brought over some fried fish, hush puppies and fries."

As soon as he opened the bag, the scent of the food drifted over to Jordan. She closed her eyes, inhaling sharply. "Smells delicious."

"Good. It won't taste as good as yours, but it won't be half bad, if I do say so myself."

Jordan chuckled.

Before Declan passed over the food, he stared at her. "How are you feeling…really?"

"I've got a bad case of cabin fever." She propped her elbow on the armrest, laying her chin in her hand. "Mike wants me to stay up here until I feel one hundred percent. But I've *rested* all week and can't take it anymore. It's like I'm Rapunzel or some other poor princess trying to escape from the tower. Only I don't have some woodland creature to keep me company or hair to aid in escape." She pointed to the short cut she'd been wearing for the past five years.

Declan grinned. "If I promise to take you somewhere you can relax, would you want to go?"

"Yes." She straightened. "Do you think the big bad wolf will let us?"

Declan laughed outright. "I think you're mixing up your fairy tales."

"I don't care, as long as you can help me bust out."

"Let's go." He stood. "I'll bring the food with me."

"Good." She *was* hungry, but that came second to wanting to spend time with Declan.

Perhaps all this time she thought she was waylaid with cabin fever was really symptoms of missing Declan. While they were out, maybe Jordan would find the courage to ask what had taken him so long to visit her.

Declan sent a thank-you heavenward, as the first exchange with Jordan went over smoothly. He hadn't had a plan when he'd received the text from Mike telling him to come over. Declan had been biding his time, trying to give Jordan a chance to heal before he dropped a huge declaration on her.

He didn't want pain from a brain injury to influence her in any way or, worse, prevent her from understanding what he had to say. So when that text appeared, he'd fried up an extra fish—he'd already been preparing lunch—and made a goody bag to bring over. It was times like these he was glad River was in school.

Once Declan had arrived, a weight he'd been carrying around all week left him. Jordan looked so much better now than she had in the hospital. Hearing how much she needed to be outdoors gave him the perfect idea to reveal his love for her.

It involved the great outdoors, good food and even better company.

He drove toward his house, thankful he'd cleaned up earlier. His back deck would make the perfect spot to relax and provide a change of scenery for Jordan.

"How is River doing?" she asked. "I miss seeing him and hearing what he has to say."

One of the reasons he loved her. *Man, that felt good to think.*

Declan glanced at her before staring back at the road. "He misses you too. At least three times a day, he asks me when you'll be better and when he can visit."

She gasped. "Is that why you haven't come by? Did you think I was too unwell to visit?"

"Kind of." He winced. "More so, I've got a five-year-old who will talk your ear off and won't understand what quiet means, because he didn't come with that setting."

She laughed softly. "I still would've liked to see him."

"Then maybe this weekend, if you still feel up to it, we can arrange something." And maybe it would be with them as an established couple. He prayed his news would make her want to see him *and* River every day for the rest of their lives.

Should he remember that when sharing his feelings, or was that too cheesy?

"Sounds great." She paused a beat. "Where are you taking me?"

"My house, if that's okay? We can stare off into the forest, relax and eat."

Jordan sighed. "I'm just happy to be out of the house. The top floor of the general store is lackluster."

Declan chuckled. "You can stay at my place as long as you want. Just take it easy, 'kay?"

"Fine. I don't imagine staring out into the forest will be too taxing," she quipped.

"Just listen to your body. I'll take you back home whenever you want a nap or whatever."

She laid a hand on his forearm. "I'm okay, and I promise I'll let you know if anything is too much."

He blew out a breath, then nodded his understanding. It would be a while before he could erase the memory of her limp body in his arms. No way Declan wanted to impede her healing process.

Soon he pulled up into his driveway. Declan grabbed the paper bag of food and led Jordan around the back.

"Should I grab plates?" he asked.

"Nah. Who needs them?"

Declan laughed. "How about I go heat this up in the oven?"

She rolled her eyes and smirked. "You and your hot food."

"You'll appreciate it when that fish crisps back up instead of being soggy." Though hopefully the foil had kept it from getting mushy.

He rushed into the house, placed the food in the oven, then rushed right back out, trying to appear calm. "I didn't think this through," he said, taking a seat in one of the Adirondack chairs.

"Think what through?" She pulled her legs up onto the seat and leaned against the back.

"What I wanted to say."

She arched an eyebrow. "What's going on? Everything okay?"

He ran a hand through his hair. "Yes. Just fine." It truly was.

His future held endless possibilities now that his feelings around Jordan had gained clarity. Not to mention his ex had dropped her request for the start-up money. Apparently, Hawk had determined they didn't need it. Instead, she would be paying child support until River turned eighteen. Declan's finances were looking up, but that wasn't the only thing that had improved.

Ballanger Advertisement had given him a glowing review, despite the mishap that had occurred on their team-building camping trip. As a result, three other companies had booked an excursion with Porter Adventures. Each company had paid half the fee up front, which would allow Declan to hire another guide.

But that news could wait. Declan had matters of the heart to settle first.

"Then what is it?" Jordan asked, pulling him from his thoughts.

"When you didn't immediately pop up after your kayak flipped, my heart stopped. When I jumped into the water to help you, my life flashed before my eyes."

"*Your* life? I thought it was supposed to be mine?" Confusion filled her eyes.

Was he muddling this? "Hear me out."

Jordan nodded.

Declan took a deep breath before jumping into an explanation. "A picture of me growing old flashed through my mind, and I was all alone. No River and no you. When I saw you were unconscious, instant regret filled me. I should've never had said we would remain just friends."

He rubbed his forehead, the memory of that day pounding fresh in his mind. Declan didn't think he'd ever forget that look on Jordan's face when he pulled her from that river or the terror in his heart.

"Having to breathe life into your lungs, doing chest compressions all brought instant clarity to me. Suddenly, my excuse of keeping my heart safe from you seemed flimsy. Because there I knelt beside your still body, praying you would live. My heart felt anything but protected." His voice cracked as his mouth dried.

"Seeing you like that and taking the time to pray for you all this past week made me realize I don't want to go another day without you in my life, without the assurance that I am yours and you are mine."

So not what he'd practiced over the past few

days, but too late to rearrange the words one more time in his mind and say them again. He took a chance and glanced at her, startled to see tears in her eyes.

"Don't cry," he whispered.

Jordan swiped at the salt tracks going down her cheeks. "They're happy tears."

"Please explain. I'm lost." But, man, he hoped that meant good things for them.

"That day, I made a promise to be your friend because that was what you needed. I told myself not to hope for more, to stay in the moment." A watery grin appeared on her sweet lips.

"Yet every time we interacted, my heart fluttered with longing." She paused. "And this past week, Declan Ames Porter, you didn't visit me, not once."

Had he been wrong in staying away? "I'm so sorry."

She held up a hand, shaking her head. "I'm not. Because it showed me how much I missed you. How much I love you. Nothing would make me happier than you being mine and me being yours."

He closed his eyes as relief swept through him. "Thank God." Declan opened his eyes to stare into her brown depths. "I love you too, Jordan Mikael Wood."

They rose to their feet simultaneously, moving into each other's arms. He cradled her head, peering into her gaze, which was locked on his. "Does this hurt?"

"It only will if you don't kiss me."

A soft chuckle escaped his lips as he lowered his face to hers. Declan softly pressed his lips against hers, testing the pressure while cataloging the feel of her mouth. Jordan stepped closer, tightening her arms around his waist.

He broke off the kiss a few moments later, reminding himself she was still recovering. "Do you feel okay?" He scanned her features, looking for any hint of pain.

"I'm perfect, Declan."

Just then, her stomach rumbled loudly.

"I don't know about that." He grinned. "Apparently you're hungry."

She laughed. "Well, yeah, but it doesn't ruin the perfectly happy feeling coursing through me right now."

"Good." He kissed the tip of her nose. "I'll get the food. You rest."

She beamed at him.

They held hands while using one hand to hold their forks, forgoing eating with their fingers as they talked of the future. Their conversation lasted well into the afternoon, until Jordan's eyes began to droop.

Declan took his time, memorizing her every

beautiful feature. The ones that made her specifically Jordan, the love of his life. He shifted and squeezed her hand. "Hey, sweetheart, time to get you home."

Her eyes flew open. She stretched, taking in her surroundings. "Do I really have to go back to the tower?" she groused.

"Yes."

She blew out a breath, then faced him. "But I'll see you tomorrow?"

"You'll see me for all my tomorrows."

Jordan laid a hand on her heart. "I think I just became the happiest woman in Willow Springs."

He laid a soft kiss on her cheek. "Then that makes me the happiest man."

Epilogue

A year later

"Mom!" River shouted.

Jordan looked up from the chopping board and toward the front hallway. River came running straight down the hall into the great room. She quickly rinsed her hands and dried them before scooping him up, noting it was getting more difficult to do so quickly.

"Did you have fun camping?" she asked.

Declan had taken River for a boys' only camping trip. They'd only gone for one night, but it had been too quiet. She missed her Porter men.

"Yes. It was the best." River kissed her cheek, then wiggled so she'd set him down. He never liked to hug very long these days.

At six years old, he'd grown a couple of

inches and leaned out some. But his cheeks remained squishable, and he still requested she read him bedtime stories.

River reached for a slice of cheese off the cutting board, all the while exclaiming how he and Declan had hiked, camped, fished and everything in between. Feeling the heat of her husband's gaze, she glanced away from River.

Declan's warm blue eyes seemed to take her in, conveying how much he missed her and that he was happy to see her. Jordan grinned, hoping her expression conveyed the same thing. She also hoped he didn't expect the surprise coming his way.

Jordan had been planning a reveal since her suspicions had been confirmed. The past couple of weeks, she'd been feeling queasy and... *different*. It wasn't just one thing, but an accumulation of little things that had her wondering if she needed to take a pregnancy test. Finally, she'd gotten up the courage to confirm her suspicions. Now she simply needed the right time to surprise her husband with the results.

However, she'd have to wait until River fell asleep, *if* she could make it until then. She wanted Declan to be the first to know and understood how important it would be to tell River at the right moment. She'd been praying all weekend Declan would be as overjoyed as she was.

A few hours later, after dinner, a bedtime routine and promises to do something as a family tomorrow, River went to bed. Jordan grabbed the little gift she'd prepared for Declan and went to find her husband. Not that he was lost. He usually sat out on the back deck and stargazed. It was his way to wind down, a routine she'd joined him in most nights since they'd married six months before.

Lord, please let him be happy. Please.

She walked out the French doors and toward the empty Adirondack chair next to Declan's. She set the gift down on the bistro table as Declan rose to his feet. He pulled her into his arms, and she wound her own around his neck.

"I missed you," he murmured.

"Missed you too."

He gave her a kiss that said *I love you, I missed you, I'm glad I'm back.*

Jordan pulled back and grinned at Declan. "It felt like y'all were gone forever."

He beamed. "I hope you'll always greet me like this when I come home."

She just laughed. "I got you a gift." She pointed to the box on the table.

"A gift?" Declan arched a brow at the box. "Aw, honey, you really did miss me."

"I did." She pointed to the box. "Now open the present, please."

He dropped a kiss on her lips, then sat down. "Thank you. I can't wait to see what it is."

Jordan was too nervous to sit. She drew in a steady breath, but her nerves were all primed to jump up and down in celebration.

But if Jordan didn't sit down, the nerves would overcome her. She took the empty chair, willing herself not to fidget as Declan took the bow off the gift box.

Next, he lifted the lid and sifted through the tissue paper. *Why is he going so slow?* She should have remembered from when his birthday had passed. It was like he had to preserve every last material that went into wrapping a present. Finally, he pulled up the baby onesie she'd bought off of Etsy. It read *Hello, Dad.* Jordan gulped as she watched Declan read the words.

His eyes widened, and then his gaze met hers. "Are you serious?"

She nodded.

His gaze dropped to her still-flat stomach. "You're pregnant?" he whispered in awe.

"I am." She cleared her throat as her eyes began to water.

"You've just made me the happiest man again, Mrs. Porter." Declan drew her to her feet, tenderly rubbing her stomach. "Hello, baby Porter."

A tear spilled down her cheek. How had God blessed her so much with the love from this man? *Thank You, Father!*

"Are you really happy?" she whispered.

"The happiest." Declan cupped her face and dipped his head to kiss her.

Jordan twined her arms around his neck, running her fingers through his hair. She'd never imagined when she first ran into Declan last spring that he'd make her feel so cherished. That her heart would feel best when they were together, knowing they could handle whatever came their way. Adding another one to their family hadn't been planned, but she was thankful Declan was as ecstati as she was.

He broke off the kiss and stared into her eyes. "Guess we're headed for another adventure, huh?"

"Is this your attempt at a dad joke?" She arched an eyebrow at him, trying to hold in her laughter at his terrible brand of humor.

"Honey, all my jokes are dad jokes."

She laughed, smacking his lips with hers. "Then it's a good thing I like your jokes."

"You can't help yourself." He wrapped her in his arms again, and Jordan let out a sigh.

"In your arms is where I always want to be."

"Then I'll make sure they're always ready for you."

Happy tears spilled over and she snuggled closer. "I love you, Mr. Porter."

"I love you more, Mrs. Porter."

At this moment, Jordan felt cocooned by his love. *Thank You for such a blessing, Lord.* She hadn't deserved the kindness of Declan. Certainly hadn't deserved the added blessing of being River's stepmom. Knowing they would add to their family had her heart practically bursting with joy.

Once again, God had shown Jordan that He was always good. Through the lows of friendships breaking up for good, the highs of marrying Declan, and today, God showed up to see her through it all. She would mark down this day to remember the many blessings, to remember when life seemed too hard to handle and Jordan was tempted to forget how much God loved her and her family. She would remember this feeling right now and all that led up to it. She would count her blessings, starting with the day Declan walked into the general store asking for help with Porter Adventures—a business that was now thriving thanks to God's goodness.

Looking back, Jordan could see *she* was the one who'd really needed help. If God hadn't shown her the lies she'd believed in her own life about her worth, then she would've never been opened to taking a chance with Declan. If

God hadn't let Jordan literally get knocked on the head, Declan wouldn't have realized how much he wanted her in his life and how great their future would be together.

Porter Adventures was flourishing, the general store was doing better than ever, and Jordan was helping more and more businesses in Willow Springs bring in more foot traffic and make their town one tourists loved to visit.

She laid her head against Declan's chest and continued counting her blessings within the comfort of her husband's arms.

* * * * *

If you enjoyed this story,
Be sure to check out

Her Christmas Redemption
by Toni Shiloh

Available now from Love Inspired!

Dear Reader,

Thank you for journeying with Jordan and Declan's story in Winning His Trust.

These two gave me a lot of difficulty in telling their story. Thanks to some good friends who encouraged me through prayer and an awesome brainstorming session, the story you have in your hands is one that fills me with gratitude. Without help and prayer, I know this story wouldn't be what it is. Isn't that just like Jordan and Declan's story? They had to understand that it's okay to be vulnerable with others. That it's okay to accept hope and, ultimately, find the Source of their help.

I pray this story encourages you in your own journey. Let the Lord direct your steps, and remember, He's placed you in a community. Take a chance to be vulnerable when you need help; you'll be amazed at the results.

If you'd like to connect with me, follow me at Facebook.com/authortonishiloh or via my website ToniShiloh.com.

Blessings,
Toni

Get 4 FREE REWARDS!

We'll send you 2 FREE Books <u>plus</u> 2 FREE Mystery Gifts.

FREE
Value Over
$20

Both the **Love Inspired®** and **Love Inspired® Suspense** series feature compelling novels filled with inspirational romance, faith, forgiveness and hope.

YES! Please send me 2 FREE novels from the Love Inspired or Love Inspired Suspense series and my 2 FREE gifts (gifts are worth about $10 retail). After receiving them, if I don't wish to receive any more books, I can return the shipping statement marked "cancel." If I don't cancel, I will receive 6 brand-new Love Inspired Larger-Print books or Love Inspired Suspense Larger-Print books every month and be billed just $6.49 each in the U.S. or $6.74 each in Canada. That is a savings of at least 16% off the cover price. It's quite a bargain! Shipping and handling is just 50¢ per book in the U.S. and $1.25 per book in Canada.* I understand that accepting the 2 free books and gifts places me under no obligation to buy anything. I can always return a shipment and cancel at any time by calling the number below. The free books and gifts are mine to keep no matter what I decide.

Choose one: ☐ **Love Inspired**   ☐ **Love Inspired Suspense**
                          Larger-Print   **Larger-Print**
                          (122/322 IDN GRHK)   (107/307 IDN GRHK)

Name (please print)

Address   Apt. #

City   State/Province   Zip/Postal Code

Email: Please check this box ☐ if you would like to receive newsletters and promotional emails from Harlequin Enterprises ULC and its affiliates. You can unsubscribe anytime.

Mail to the **Harlequin Reader Service:**
IN U.S.A.: P.O. Box 1341, Buffalo, NY 14240-8531
IN CANADA: P.O. Box 603, Fort Erie, Ontario L2A 5X3

Want to try 2 free books from another series? Call 1-800-873-8635 or visit www.ReaderService.com.

Get 4 FREE REWARDS!

We'll send you 2 FREE Books plus <u>2</u> FREE Mystery Gifts.

FREE
Value Over
$20

Both the **Harlequin® Special Edition** and **Harlequin® Heartwarming™** series feature compelling novels filled with stories of love and strength where the bonds of friendship, family and community unite.

YES! Please send me 2 FREE novels from the Harlequin Special Edition or Harlequin Heartwarming series and my 2 FREE gifts (gifts are worth about $10 retail). After receiving them, if I don't wish to receive any more books, I can return the shipping statement marked "cancel." If I don't cancel, I will receive 6 brand-new Harlequin Special Edition books every month and be billed just $5.49 each in the U.S. or $6.24 each in Canada, a savings of at least 12% off the cover price, or 4 brand-new Harlequin Heartwarming Larger-Print books every month and be billed just $6.24 each in the U.S. or $6.74 each in Canada, a savings of at least 19% off the cover price. It's quite a bargain! Shipping and handling is just 50¢ per book in the U.S. and $1.25 per book in Canada.* I understand that accepting the 2 free books and gifts places me under no obligation to buy anything. I can always return a shipment and cancel at any time by calling the number below. The free books and gifts are mine to keep no matter what I decide.

Choose one: ☐ **Harlequin Special Edition**   ☐ **Harlequin Heartwarming**
(235/335 HDN GRJV)   **Larger-Print**
                            (161/361 HDN GRJV)

Name (please print)

Address   Apt. #

City   State/Province   Zip/Postal Code

Email: Please check this box ☐ if you would like to receive newsletters and promotional emails from Harlequin Enterprises ULC and its affiliates. You can unsubscribe anytime.

Mail to the **Harlequin Reader Service:**
IN U.S.A.: P.O. Box 1341, Buffalo, NY 14240-8531
IN CANADA: P.O. Box 603, Fort Erie, Ontario L2A 5X3

Want to try 2 free books from another series? Call 1-800-873-8635 or visit www.ReaderService.com.

*Terms and prices subject to change without notice. Prices do not include sales taxes, which will be charged (if applicable) based on your state or country of residence. Canadian residents will be charged applicable taxes. Offer not valid in Quebec. This offer is limited to one order per household. Books received may not be as shown. Not valid for current subscribers to the Harlequin Special Edition or Harlequin Heartwarming series. All orders subject to approval. Credit or debit balances in a customer's account(s) may be offset by any other outstanding balance owed by or to the customer. Please allow 4 to 6 weeks for delivery. Offer available while quantities last.

Your Privacy—Your information is being collected by Harlequin Enterprises ULC, operating as Harlequin Reader Service. For a complete summary of the information we collect, how we use this information and to whom it is disclosed, please visit our privacy notice located at corporate.harlequin.com/privacy-notice. From time to time we may also exchange your personal information with reputable third parties. If you wish to opt out of this sharing of your personal information, please visit readerservice.com/consumerschoice or call 1-800-873-8635. **Notice to California Residents**—Under California law, you have specific rights to control and access your data. For more information on these rights and how to exercise them, visit corporate.harlequin.com/california-privacy.

HSEHW22R3

COUNTRY LEGACY COLLECTION

Cowboys, adventure and romance await you in this new collection! Enjoy superb reading all year long with books by bestselling authors like Diana Palmer, Sasha Summers and Marie Ferrarella!

YES! Please send me the **Country Legacy Collection!** This collection begins with 3 FREE books and 2 FREE gifts in the first shipment. Along with my 3 free books, I'll also get 3 more books from the **Country Legacy Collection**, which I may either return and owe nothing or keep for the low price of $24.60 U.S./$28.12 CDN each plus $2.99 U.S./$7.49 CDN for shipping and handling per shipment*. If I decide to continue, about once a month for 8 months, I will get 6 or 7 more books but will only pay for 4. That means 2 or 3 books in every shipment will be FREE! If I decide to keep the entire collection, I'll have paid for only 32 books because 19 are FREE! I understand that accepting the 3 free books and gifts places me under no obligation to buy anything. I can always return a shipment and cancel at any time. My free books and gifts are mine to keep no matter what I decide.

☐ 275 HCK 1939   ☐ 475 HCK 1939

Name (please print)

Address   Apt. #

City   State/Province   Zip/Postal Code

Mail to the Harlequin Reader Service:
IN U.S.A.: P.O. Box 1341, Buffalo, NY 14240-8571
IN CANADA: P.O. Box 603, Fort Erie, Ontario L2A 5X3
